COFFEE IN THE MORNING

GLADYS GREENAWAY

Coffee in the Morning

HURST & BLACKETT

HURST & BLACKETT LTD
178–202 Great Portland Street, London W1

AN IMPRINT OF THE HUTCHINSON GROUP

London Melbourne Sydney
Auckland Bombay Toronto
Johannesburg New York

First published 1967

365618

823

365618

*This book has been set in Pilgrim, printed in Great Britain
on Antique Wove paper by Anchor Press, and
bound by Wm. Brendon, both of Tiptree, Essex*

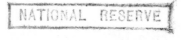

1

Jeff watched the land slip slowly out of sight before he turned away and rested his back against the rail, shoulders hunched, eyes glistening with unshed tears and his whole attitude one of wearied resignation. He didn't want to go to England, he didn't want to leave the island, he didn't want to leave Lucy and the children. He could picture them standing on the shore watching the ship disappear, just as he had watched the land fade from sight, but what else could he do? Wait until the paper folded up and left him without a job? Things were bad at home and didn't look like getting better. There wasn't much hope for a writer there. In England there were so many national, local and provincial papers. He would soon get a job and before long he would send for Lucy and the children. If only he was sure he had done the right thing. It was the first time in his life he had ever made a strong decision. Mainly things had just come his way without striving too hard, without worrying too much, but this had been almost forced on him.

At least Lucy and the children would be all right. His mother had been against the whole idea until she saw he had made up his mind, and then, like the great-hearted woman she was, had done everything possible to help. She and his father had taken Lucy and the children to live with them.

'This house is too big for your father and me. It'll be fine to have the children around, and then, if you want to go back to teaching, Lucy, they won't be any trouble to me. Haven't enough to do these days.'

So Lucy was going back to teaching and their own house had been let to an elderly English couple who had come to the island for a holiday and decided to stay on indefinitely. All this had taken a load off his mind. Lucy loved teaching and had talked about going back as soon as the children were a little older.

Dear Lucy, what a tower of strength she had been! Encouraging, helpful, never complaining, and now she would be hoping and praying that before too long they would be together again. The last days had gone so quickly, all too quickly. Giving his resignation to the *Vanguard*, arranging about the house and then the packing. Small Mandy, not yet three, had been bewildered by all the hustle and bustle. Watching him pack had been an exciting game in which she had joined with gusto, running backwards and forwards, putting things in his trunk and taking them out again; her own toys, household goods, even a plate or two, and they all had to be taken out again when she wasn't looking. Stella had wept bitterly in those last moments, but at five tears and laughter are never far away, particularly with Stella, who was a volatile soul. Steven, at seven, was made of sterner stuff and had shut his lips tightly and looked at his father out of dry eyes. Mandy had waved her hands cheerfully from the safety of her grandfather's strong arms.

The island had never looked so beautiful as in those last moments. The tree-decked hills, the white sands and glittering sea. Dear God, when would he see it again?

If only he knew what the outcome of it would be. How could anyone know? The only thing he could do was to

6

hope and pray, but his prayers were vague and didn't seem much use.

He had taken passage tourist in order to hoard his money, but at the thought of going down to the dormitory his soul cringed. He almost wished he had risked the extra now, so that he could have a little privacy. When at last he nerved himself to go below the other men were full of gaiety, singing a popular number and passing round a bottle of rum. Four of them were already engaged by London Transport and the others had friends or relations to go to. He was the odd man out in every way. Jeff Anderson, newspaper man, journalist, a man who intended to do a great deal but hadn't done much so far. Thirty-five, with the book he had meant to write years ago not even started. Nothing of any substance at the back of him, no degree which might have stood him in good stead now. Just a certain facility with words which had been partly his downfall, for it had made him lazy. Stopped him fighting.

He lay on his bunk and tried to imagine the hum of Fleet Street. If only he could feel sure he would get a job, but, as the land had vanished from sight, some of his bright hopes had fled. From the bottom of his heart he wished he had something more solid behind him than just his scrapbook of cuttings. Was Fleet Street as overcrowded as rumour had it? He had got to make good somehow. Oh Lord, think of something else or he would be rushing on deck, flinging himself overboard and trying to swim home.

When he had first conceived the idea of going to England he had been full of enthusiasm. It was the one chance to make something of himself. What chance was there on a tiny island to show his capabilities? They hadn't even a publishing house. No, England was the land of opportunity for a writer. So many publishers, so many newspapers, so many magazines!

7

Parting with Lucy had been a far greater wrench than he had thought it would be. The very fact that he had made up his mind that it would not be for long should have made it far easier, but it didn't. They had loved each other since they were in their early twenties and accepted it without realising how much they belonged to, how much they needed, each other. It wasn't until last night he had really known. He had taken her in his arms fully intending that it should be a night of tenderness and gentle talk, but as soon as he felt her warm, loving body close to him passion overruled everything. He couldn't take her enough, knew he exhausted her with his love, but it had gone on and on in desperation at the thought of the coming parting, and afterwards they had both been too worn-out for him to say any of the tender things he had in his heart and mind. Now he hated himself for having let the moments go. He had wanted to pour out his love in utter tenderness, to tell her of his deep and abiding love, of the fact that no other woman could ever take him from her even in a brief, passing thought. And he had said nothing. He, who could find words at the end of his finger-tips, could find none for that and now it was too late and his soul ached with unhappiness. Loving her with his body had been the only way he could express himself and Lucy hadn't understood. He knew that, for her eyes had been full of pain, as if the closeness of their bodies had added to the grief of parting rather than eased it. Did she think that in that last night he had only wanted sex-satisfaction? The thought was a physical pain. She meant so much more.

Why, why in all the years had he never told her how deep and strong was his love? He was appalled at how little appreciation he had shown. Why had he imagined that providing her with a good home was enough? He had enjoyed his life, enjoyed his work and accepted what came his way without diving too deep below the surface. It had all been so simple until the rumour that the *Vanguard* might have to close and he had been forced to think of the future. He knew the circulation had been falling and that of the *Sun* going up, but he had not thought it as bad as that. He knew, too, that it was useless to try to get on the *Sun*. They had their own men and although he was reasonably good he was not as good as that. He'd worked hard but not hard enough and to take him on they would have had to push another man out. No, he wouldn't wish that. If he had only had the sense to take his father's advice. Get those degrees, write a book, prove himself, instead of jogging along and letting life take care of itself. Now he would have to stir himself. Have to show that he could do more than just be a useful member of the staff on a paper that was steadily going downhill. Have to prove to his father that he had a son who was not merely a drifter. Have to prove to Lucy that he could make something of himself.

Not that his father had ever said a great deal. It had taken his mother to do that!

'Time you did more than just work on that paper, son. Time you started on that book you once bragged you were going to write. The book that was going to set the place alight. Going to make a film and everything, wasn't it?' Her voice was biting.

'That paper pays me good money, Mamma, and I don't have any time.'

'Rubbish! If you want to do a thing you can make time. You find enough time to do the things you want to do. And what about Lucy? All the things you said you were going to do for her. And what have you done? Just where you were when you married her. Sometimes I think your papa was wrong when he let you have your own way. He wanted you to study hard and be a lawyer or a doctor, but

9

no, you wouldn't do anything like that. You were going to be a writer. Going to set the town on fire. Not like your father, just a teacher!'

It was one of Mamma's scolding days. He had called in to see how she was on his way home and he didn't know that she had already heard the rumours about the *Vanguard*. She must have been worrying about his future and that of Lucy and the children.

'Sometimes I think your papa should have taken a strap to you and made you work. He's too easy, that man.'

He smiled a little at the memory of those words. The thought of his father taking a strap to anyone was funny. Such a big, gentle man with nothing in his heart but love. He loved God with a deep faith that was as certain as the sun was in the heavens. He loved his wife with a deep, abiding love. He loved his family, his son, his two daughters, his sons-in-law and his daughter-in-law and his grandchildren. He loved his pupils, too, and handled them with love and encouragement, never with fear. He couldn't have taken a strap or a cane to anyone, much less his only son. Perhaps, though, his mother had been right. It would have been better had he been tougher. Forced him to settle down to study rather than play around with words. No doubt his father had thought that in the long run he would play around with them to a purpose instead of remaining just a member of the staff, turning his hand to anything that happened along.

Dear God, he was going to miss his parents! They had been a sheet-anchor all his days. No use thinking about what had gone, better make up his mind to make something worth while of the future.

The other men were still laughing and talking. Quietly he got out of his bunk and went towards the door.

'Say, where you going, man?'

He forced a grin. 'Where do you think? Do you want to go for me?' There was a burst of laughter.

He went on deck and leant on the rail. Darkness closed its arms round him like a warm blanket. The moon sailed on a cloudless sky. Unaccustomed tears trickled down his dark face and he brushed them aside with the back of his hand irritably. If he wasn't careful he would become more woman than man, but how could he face the coming days?

They went by slowly, draggingly, until he thought they would never end. He made efforts to be friendly with the other men but failed, hopelessly. There was no meeting point and it gave him a sense of shame. He should be able to meet them on their own ground. Call himself a writer! It was then that he realised that people who made the news had been news to him rather than people. He had never made an effort to find out what made them tick. All he had been interested in was what had happened. Perhaps that was why he had never written that book. He had never tried to understand people. Or perhaps it was because so little happened on the island apart from politics and who wanted to read about them except in a newspaper? To write a book one needed experience, experience outside the island. In England there would be so much to see, so much to do, ideas would flow. How could he have ever expected to write that book on a tiny island where nothing every happened? He needed this change. He should have made it long ago. Once he was settled, had got work on a newspaper, he would write that book. In England there would be more time.

His unharnessed dreams romped ahead. The book was written, a film made, his name established. Lucy and the children were living with him in a charming house outside London. His parents came over on a holiday. They were all going back to the island for a visit and he was no longer Jeff Anderson of the *Vanguard* but Jeff Anderson, the well-known author. It was a lovely dream and carried him to the shores of what he was sure would be the land of success.

It wasn't until he was through the Customs that he realised he had nowhere to go and had turned down the offer of help from an official-looking Jamaican. He hated to admit to anyone that he needed help.

He put his luggage in the left-luggage office and bought a paper. It was early and he had plenty of time. There were pages and pages of adverts for jobs which looked hopeful. There were also pages of cars for sale, but his immediate need was for somewhere to stay. Not even a small column of rooms or boarding houses. Clearly he had the wrong paper. He went back to the bookstall and bought an advertising paper. He also bought an A to Z. In the snack bar he had a coffee and a sandwich and sat down to work things out. Try the places near the station, to start with.

It was astonishing at how many houses with 'Rooms to Let' in the window that he was told, reasonably politely, they were sorry, the card had been left in the window by mistake. They were full. One woman looked at him quite frankly, said 'No coloureds!' and closed the door. At one house he waited to see if the card was taken out of the window, but it wasn't. This was something he hadn't expected. He went on trying with dogged persistence and the day got later and later and his feet were lead in his shoes and his heart a stone in his tired body. He had forgotten his loneliness, his longing for his family, and above all for Lucy, in a hopeless weariness that was like nothing he had ever experienced before. His spirit seemed to have left his body and he was an empty shell that walked and walked, rang bells, knocked knockers and saw doors open and shut.

I'll have to go to the police, he thought, I can't go on much longer. Just try once more. He knew he was at the end of his tether. He had gone off the beaten track and was in a street of rundown houses, most of them with peeling paintwork and faded curtains. He didn't even realise that the one at which he knocked had no card in the window.

After a few minutes the door opened. A little woman stood in front of him, bent back, wrinkled face, worn hands folded in front of a snowy, old-fashioned apron.

'Have you a room to let, please?'

She looked at his huge figure with the drooping shoulders, then up at his tired face. Her blue eyes were shrewd but kindly.

'Lord love us, there's no rooms to let here. This is all let off in flats and every blessed one full.'

He leant against the wall and said nothing, but his whole body had the hopeless look of a dog that has been turned out on a wet, cold night with no knowledge of where he could find shelter.

'Come on in and I'll give you a cuppa. My old man and me's just going to have one.'

He followed her down some backstairs to a basement without using thought at all. It was the first friendly face he had seen. If she had said she would take him down to a thieves' kitchen he would have gone with her. Sitting by an old-fashioned, open fire was an old man. His scanty hair was brushed neatly over his head and he was in his shirt sleeves, his braces dangling round his skinny thighs.

'This chap wants a room. Didn't even notice all the bells and nobody here would answer the knocker 'cept me. Sit down, man, you look fair whacked.'

'Thank you.' The words were little more than a whisper. The old armchair looked as if it would collapse under his weight, but it held and was astonishingly comfortable.

'Come on, you drink this. Nothing like a cuppa tea to cheer you up.'

It was bitter-strong and very sweet, nothing like the tea he was used to drinking but it was nectar from the gods. He sipped it, letting the quiet and warmth of the clean but shabby room and the kindly faces of the old people wrap him round like a benison. A lump rose in his throat. Just when he felt all hope had gone he had met with this. The fact that he still had nowhere to sleep no longer mattered. Neither of the old people spoke while he was drinking. They waited with the patience and gentleness of an older generation. When he had finished the old lady took the cup and saucer from his hand.

'Been tramping for hours by the look of you. Tried all the wrong places, too, like as not. Only got in today, I suppose?'

'Thought there was always someone to meet you people and show you the ropes.' The old man shook his head as if the world was a sorry place.

A faint grin flickered across Jeff's dark face.

'So there was but I was too clever and thought I could manage by myself. I didn't realise the difficulties.'

'And no friends in London?'

'No.'

'Bit of a mug, aren't you?' But the words were kindly, not disparaging.

'More than a bit. Thank you for the tea, it's put new life into me. Can you tell me where I could get a room for tonight?'

'Not offhand. Too late to find one, but I'll have a go in the morning.'

The sudden despair on the dark face made the old man grin.

'Coo, don't get yourself all steamed up. Me and the

14

missus won't turn you out. You can kip down there on the sofa.' He looked at the big figure critically. 'You won't never make it! We'll make up a bed on the floor. Won't be soft, but better than the pavement.' He grinned again. 'Not that the police would let you.'

It was a night Jeff would never forget. Alfred and Lizzie Jones fed him on bread and cheese and pickles with a slab of homemade cake afterwards and more strong, sweet tea. Then they made him up a bed on the floor and he slept, deep, dreamless, health-giving sleep, and when he wakened, puzzled for a moment by his strange surroundings, the memory of their kindness was balm to his soul. As soon as he was settled, as soon as he had a room, he must write home and tell them of the unexpected kindness of two old people to a wanderer in a strange and apparently unfriendly land.

They insisted on him eating a breakfast large enough for two and then old Alfred said he was off to work.

'Potman, I am, along at the Rose and Crown. Now you stay here, son, along o' Lizzie and I'll ask around if they know someone what's got a room. Mind you, it's not going to be easy. Most of 'em are full up and some of 'em won't take anyone what's coloured. This is a funny sort of neighbourhood, like. The more classy places is choosy and the cheaper ones full. Never mind, we'll find something.'

He came back after midday closing with triumph written all over him.

'It ain't exactly the Ritz and it's not permanent, but then I don't think you'd want it to be, but it's clean enough. Doris Burton's son's gone away up north—at least, that's what she says. If I know her Reggie he's in stir for a few months, but Doris is all right and she'll be jolly glad of a lodger for a bit. She'll be a lot better off than with that scallywag of a son.'

15

Alf took him to a little back street of tiny cottages that were due for demolition when the council got around to it. In the meantime they were still occupied. Jeff could hardly believe it was possible that such places existed in London, but obviously they did.

Doris Burton eyed him up and down and then grinned.

'Alf was right. This ain't the sort of place you've bin used to, but it's better than nothing until you find something else. I'll show you your room and tomorrow you can get your luggage.'

If anything the furniture was even older and shabbier than that in Alf and Lizzie's basement flat, but Alf was right, it was spotlessly clean. Jeff wondered how in the world he was going to manage with no bathroom, but before he could think too much about it Doris answered the unasked question.

'You can fetch yourself up hot water.' Then he saw the old-fashioned washstand with the pitcher and basin. 'Easy enough to put a saucepan on the stove and I don't care how much you bring up as long as I don't have to bring it. Those stairs ain't wide enough for me to run up and down.' Her fat form shook like a jelly with almost silent laughter. ' 'Course, you can always have a wash at the kitchen sink and if you want a real soak there's the public baths down the road. Oh, don't worry, they're ever so nice and clean. Go there myself once in a while.'

She would give him breakfast and an evening meal, but that was all because she had a cleaning job herself.

Jeff would never have thought it possible to fit in under the circumstances, but fit in he did. Doris explained carefully that it was only a temporary arrangement because she didn't know exactly how long her Reggie would be away. Alf told him that Reggie's case had not yet come up, but he reckoned he'd get six months.

'In and out of quod all the time. Never anything big, you know. Just petty stuff, but Doris likes to say he's gone away to work. She knows we know all about it but we pretend we don't. She feels better that way.'

Doris fed him enormous meals of starchy food and he found that all he needed midday was a cup of coffee and some fruit. Any more starch would have choked him. He fetched his luggage and hung his clothes in the rickety wardrobe, wondering where Doris had hidden her Reggie's clothes until he realised she had given him her own bedroom. He stacked his books on the floor out of the way and put his typewriter on the chest of drawers. He wished there was a table so he could type, but there would be nowhere to put it, for there was barely enough room for him to ease his big frame round the bed. When Doris discovered he had a typewriter and wanted to use it she gave him the freedom of 'the front room'. Here the furniture was even more crowded, but there was a table and chairs and the table was as solid as a rock.

'Nice, ain't it?' Doris patted the table as if it were alive and could feel her affectionate hand. 'My dad was a carpenter and 'e made it for me when I was married.'

Jeff thought her father would have been wiser to make it a bit smaller, but perhaps he had thought that at some time Doris would move on to more roomy quarters.

'You can put your typewriter 'ere and leave it. There won't be no one to touch it. Never used this room since me 'usband's funeral.'

Jeff wrote to Lucy and told her he had found somewhere to live with a very kindly landlady. He had intended to tell her of his long trek to find shelter, but thought better of it. No sense in worrying her. Neither did he tell her of the poor locality or the lack of a bathroom. He did say that his landlady was a fat, jolly woman who gave him two

17

meals a day and they would have been big enough for two men of his size and that she was charging him far less than he expected. Then, having told her the news, he poured out his heart in love.

Now there was the problem of finding work to be faced. There were all the adverts in the Tube stations and on the buses about the right papers to buy to get the best jobs. There were pages of situations vacant. Everything was needed. Hospital porters, filing clerks, storekeepers, engineers, draughtsmen, typists and executive grades, but nowhere was there a mention of reporters. Printers were in great demand. He read the papers from back to front and felt like a green youngster looking for his first job with no knowledge as to how to set about it. He had learned everything he could about England and present conditions but it seemed he knew nothing. How did one get work in Fleet Street? Did you take your courage in one hand and your cuttings in the other and beard editors in their dens? He didn't know and he had no one to ask. Why had he been so independent when that confounded Jamaican from the welfare department or wherever it was had asked if he needed help? Because, he told himself, I am a big-head and was certain I could manage alone. Official or no official he might have given him a few tips.

Doris came in while he was searching the situations vacant column of the last paper. Her eyes were sympathetic.

'Looking for a job?' He nodded. 'Plenty about but it depends what you want. What did you do at 'ome?'

'I worked on a newspaper.'

'Do you mean a printer?'

He shook his head and gave her a sudden smile. 'Anything but. I reported, I wrote columns, I even stood in for the editor at times, but it doesn't look as if anyone like that is needed.'

'Oh Lord, I don't know nothink about that. Why don't you go to the library? You might find somethink there and you won't 'ave to pay for the papers.'

Clearly Doris knew the need for saving pennies. It was something he hadn't thought about, but newspapers did mount up.

'When do they close?'

'I don't know. Never go there meself. Not that you want to go there tonight. What you want is somethink inside you, then you can look at the telly. Not that it's much of a set, mind you. Bought it secondhand, but it's somethink to do when I've got five minutes.'

Obediently he ate the meal she provided and watched the telly, although he had the greatest job to keep his eyes open. He was scarcely aware that Doris was becoming the mother figure on which he leant for comfort as he had done on his own mother and, later, Lucy. He had done what he wanted to do and yet always turned to them for love and succour, not even realising he had done little for them.

The following morning Doris gave him minute instructions as to where he could find the library. It was old, vast and gloomy, but there were armchairs in the reading room. He read the nationals from front to back and got nowhere. A couple of old men sat and snored. He wondered if they had come to read and fallen asleep with the weakness of old age or if they came because it was warm and comfortable and they had nowhere else to go. Then he found *World Press News*. Joy of joys, there was an advert for a junior reporter on a daily. A junior at his age? Well, he had to start somewhere. He wrote down the details, dashed back to No. 5 Wessex Row, grabbed his briefcase with his cuttings, looked up his A to Z carefully to make sure he would not get lost on the way, and was off.

The uniformed commissionaire stared at him doubtfully when he said he wanted to see the editor, but his well-cut suit, spotless shirt and quiet manner meant he could be someone of importance.

'Have you an appointment, sir?'

'No, I'm afraid not, but it is important.' He had no idea why he didn't say outright that he wanted a job. Perhaps some sixth sense warned him it was better to withhold that information.

'What did you say your name is, sir?'

'I didn't.' Jeff smiled. 'It's Jeffrey Anderson from Malagai.' He said it firmly, as if the name might mean something.

'Well, I don't know if the editor will be able to see you himself, he's a very busy man, but I'll put you on to some-one who will help.'

He went off to the phone and came back a few minutes later.

'Mr. Robertson will send someone down for you shortly, sir. Just take a seat.'

Jeff sank to pigmy size. If the library had seemed large this was enormous, the opening to a rabbit warren of corri-dors, lifts and what-have-you. Men and women hurried in and out, lifts clanged, doors slammed. A man with a bowler hat and a rolled umbrella dashed towards a lift and the gates closed as he reached it. The lift rose and the man swore gently. A young woman came through the swing doors, gave a 'Hullo, Craddock,' to the commissionaire, looked at Jeff curiously, smiled and went on her way, swallowed up in the vast building. Everyone had some-where to go, knew what they were doing and Jeff would have given anything to have been one of them. He waited. A long, long quarter of an hour went by while his courage sank lower and lower.

Gordon Robertson was looking at his assistant pathetically.

'Now who the heck do you think this Jeffrey Anderson is? I know by the way Craddock spoke that he could be someone important from one of the smaller islands. Has he come with a bitter complaint he wants to air about the way his fellow countrymen are being treated? Is he someone of importance we have slipped up on? Old Firecrackers is in a right mood today and if I dare ask him if he has time to see him and he turns out to be just another West Indian with a bee in his bonnet my life won't be worth living; if he is important and I don't tell him I'll be in the soup again. There's been too much publicity about racial prejudice of late and we've got to handle the situation with kid gloves or there'll be more trouble and I'm busy. Lord, why didn't I take up banking—or window-cleaning?' He stopped, looked thoughtful, and gave one of his rare smiles. 'What a job! I wonder all writers don't try it for a while.'

'If I bring him up you can find out, can't you? You're like my wife when she gets a letter in a strange handwriting. She stands and looks at it and wonders who it is from when all she has to do is to open the envelope.' Ned Fowler sighed. 'If it's about the case of the coloured family being treated rough because they were offered a council house you can fob him off by telling him we've got a man on the job.'

'O.K. Let me finish going over this article by old Farrow and then I'll see the bloke. Old Farrow gets his facts but I wish to heaven he didn't use so many bloody adjectives.'

He looked up as Jeff was shown into the office. The man

had a certain quiet presence. Dress good, kinky hair cut short, eyes steady if slightly anxious. Was he news, did he have news or was he just a bloody nuisance?

'Sit down, Mr. Anderson. My name is Robertson, Gordon Robertson. I'm Mr. Bennett's assistant. I'm afraid he's engaged at the moment. Can I help you?' His manner gave no indication of his thoughts.

'I've come about this job you advertise for a junior reporter.'

The accent was strong but pleasant and the voice good. Was this a gag? Was he someone on the political racket trying to prove race prejudice even on a newspaper where they seemed more or less eager to assist the black angels? Hell, he'd have to tread warily. He didn't like it, not one bit.

'Not for yourself?' Robertson gave a pleasant smile.

'You mean because it is for a junior?'

'Yes.'

'I have to start somewhere and there seem no other posts open.'

'That is a bit of a problem, isn't it? You see most of our people start as cubs or come in from the provinces after a great deal of experience. They work up gradually.'

'I realise that is the case. It's much the same back home. Here I'm a new boy all over again.'

'What experience have you had?'

Jeff opened his briefcase and took out a scrapbook. 'I was on the *Vanguard* for twelve years and during that time I did anything and almost everything apart from printing it myself. Before that I was on the *Watchman* for five years, but that folded up.'

Gordon Robertson stared at him. Good God, the man was genuine after all, or it appeared so. But be wary, even now there could be a catch in it. Never trust anyone, was his motto, not until you had proved they were genuine beyond a doubt. He could have already written an article for a rival, showing that their policy of being fair to coloured immigrants was largely phony. It was tricky. He glanced through the cuttings. Not bad. Not always up to standard but whose were? The man had an eye for news, and the writing was better than some he had seen even in the nationals.

He looked across at Jeff with weary eyes. If he was an Englishman, a Scotsman or an Irishman it would be easy. He could say right out that it was not the job for him, but he couldn't be so open with a coloured man. There could be a lot of backwash. Their own policy was too well known. Fair treatment in every case, regardless of colour. Let that dirty little red rag, the *Comet*, get hold of the fact that a job was going that this man could do on his head and he had turned him down and their name would be mud. Why did colour matter so much? He didn't care a damn about a man's skin, but here he was having to lean over backwards in order not to cause trouble or give offence. Christ, if only one could be natural for a change and not care tuppence what anyone thought! Suppose he did offer him the job? How could a man of his age work under a little slob like Dukes, who enjoyed humiliating anyone?

'How long have you been over here, Mr. Anderson?'

'A week.'

Robertson breathed a sigh of relief. Surely in that time nobody could have got hold of him? Damn, a week was plenty of time.

'Have you tried any other papers?'

'No, there hasn't been much time yet, but naturally I want to start work as soon as possible.'

Robertson was certain the man was telling the truth,

but it was still tricky. If only the blasted job was filled. It would make it so much easier. Suddenly he saw a way out.

'Mr. Anderson, I'm going to be frank with you. Getting a job as a reporter these days is not easy. Just as a great number of girls think they can act and want to be stars of stage or screen, so a tremendous amount of people think they can write, and a good many can, but both professions are decidedly overcrowded. There are plenty of jobs going in almost every other walk of life but not in these two. If you were a youngster I would take you on and you could sink or swim according to your efforts and your ability, but not at your age for a very good reason. It might be years before you could crawl out of the rut and your work would suffer. During the short time you have been in England what has been your reaction? Good, bad or indifferent?'

Jeff's smile broke out and his eyes twinkled with amusement. Robertson found himself liking the man and hoping he would get what he wanted.

'Quite extraordinary and like nothing I expected.'

'Then go back to wherever you are living and write me an article. I promise you it will have my personal attention and if it is not exactly what I want I will tell you why. I would rather it was not too damning about any treatment you have had. We prefer that to come from a white man You may not know much about our paper but we are making an effort to improve racial relations. Free-lancing is a tough job. If you make the grade it is rewarding and reasonably well paid. It is a far better bet for you than to try and get on the staff of a newspaper. Let me make it clear, too, that I am not commissioning this article but I will accept it if you have the right approach.'

'Thank you, Mr. Robertson. That is a kind and generous offer and I will do my best.'

'And don't think if we take this article you will then be able to earn a living straight away as a free-lance. One swallow never made a summer yet and I'm warning you. If I were in your shoes I'd take a job, any ruddy job I could get, and write in my spare time. It's a bloody hard life but if you are a writer you'll do it.' He gave Jeff a grin and held out his hand. 'Good luck and you can bring the article in yourself. I'll leave word that you can come up.

'And let that bloody article be good,' Robertson muttered as the door closed. 'I've got a feeling that it may be, but if it is I only hope it doesn't raise the poor bugger's hopes too high. Might be six months before he sells another, if ever.'

Jeff went back to Wessex Row with his heart high and full of gratitude. This was his chance and he would make full use of it. Oh, bless Doris Burton's sweet soul for suggesting the library.

He was still full of elation when he sat down to his typewriter the next morning. He was typing furiously when he realised the article was brimming over with his present feelings. This was not a true writer's work. He was letting those first hours of loneliness, misery and exhaustion slip away. They were the beginning and the beginning was important. If only he knew something of the paper's policy. No, that wouldn't do. It would colour the article with what they wanted rather than his own experience. He tore up what he had written and started again. He longed for coffee. Lucy's rich, brown coffee, pungent-smelling, rich and sweet. Coffee was something that did not exist for Doris, not even the instant kind. He could go out and get some. No, make a cup of tea.

He had written nothing he could feel satisfied about and he began to panic. Somehow he could not recapture those first hours when utter despair had almost swamped him. They had slipped away from him in the kindliness of three old people and a tough assistant editor. It wouldn't do. He tore everything up again. Sitting with his elbows on the table he put his hands to his short-cropped hair and scratched vigorously as if that would put the right thoughts in his head. The most idiotic longing for coffee tore at him. It was like the yearning for a woman's arms. The only coffee he had had since he arrived had been in a coffee bar, so he might just as well try it again.

He looked out at the grim street, seeing it clearly for the first time. A cold drizzle looked as if it had settled for ever. Get out and walk. Clear his brain and have that coffee. He put on his raincoat and walked for an hour. Up one street and down another, trying to recapture his first feelings, but for some reason they eluded him. Then the smell of coffee filled his nostrils. He sniffed appreciatively and paused.

The coffee bar was fairly clean, the girl behind the counter, her hair bleached to a pale blonde, dark at the roots, gave him a pert smile.

'Hullo, Handsome, what do you want?'

It was deliberately provocative and made him feel slightly stupid.

'Just a cup of coffee.'

She brought it and then put her skinny arms on the counter.

'Never seen you before. Lived here long?'

'Not long.'

'Don't talk much, do you?' Her grin showed sharp little teeth. To Jeff there was something positively repulsive about her. The heavy make-up round her pale eyes, the almost white lipstick and those sharp little teeth, her narrow, pointed nose and the pallid, unhealthy complexion, as if no sun had ever coloured her cheeks or brought warmth to her mouth. Something from the underworld! He found himself smiling at his own imagination.

'That's better. Time I had a smile.'

She was openly making a pass at him and he had no idea why. No sense in being unfriendly, but drink his coffee and get out. It tasted good after so much thick tea. His smile was easier.

'Sorry I seemed unfriendly but I'm a bit tired.'

'And you'd better remain unfriendly.' His elbow was pushed and some of the coffee went down his suit. 'You leave my girl alone. We don't want your sort here. Go home, nigger.'

An ungainly youth stood at his side, eyes smouldering and hands clenched. Jeff looked at him with something close to contempt in his dark eyes, but his voice was quiet, dangerously quiet.

'Then, if she is your girl you had better keep an eye on her, hadn't you? Hers are inclined to wander.' He knew now that her manner had merely been a goad to lash the boy's jealousy and, in spite of his anger, there was a little pity.

'You dirty sod! I'll get you for that sometime.'

Jeff smiled, knowing full well he could have broken the stripling in two.

'You're welcome to try, any time.'

'What's going on?' A man came from the room at the back. 'I'm not having any trouble here.'

'Don't worry, you won't.' Jeff had lost his taste for coffee. He moved away from the counter slowly. The first day, the closed doors, the aching legs and heart were back with him like a dark cloud hemming him in. He walked out of the place with shoulders back, determinedly indifferent but feeling the hate that followed him like something solid.

'You make up to one of them dirty blacks again, Maisie, and I'll do you, honest to God I will.'

'Oh, shut up. I was just having him on. A bit soft, they are. Anyone would think I was asking him to go to bed with me to hear you. I wouldn't let one of them touch me.'

'You'd better not.'

The high-pitched voices carried into the street. So, thought Jeff, you mustn't be friendly and you mustn't be unfriendly. Where do we stand? The swish of a broom made him turn and he saw one of his own colour sweeping the gutter. A cloth cap was pulled down over his ears, his eyes bent on the ground. Was his mind on his task or was it back on some sunny, sandy beach? Was he any better off here than he would have been on his own island? Jeff wanted to speak, to give him some word of cheer, but he couldn't—not after the last few minutes.

He went back to Wessex Row and no sooner had the door closed behind him than he again wanted coffee, but this time it was with a deep homesickness which was not so much the need of coffee but of his own people. He made himself a cup of tea and went back to his typewriter. The knowledge that his future might stand or fall by this article didn't help. He wanted to get it done quickly, to take it to Robertson and let him see he was willing to work, but the tension grew and grew until he thought he would never be able to cope with words or thoughts again. Time and time again he was tempted to go out and get a copy of the *Meteor* but he wouldn't let himself. It must be his own style or it would never ring true. When Doris came home he was still at it. She saw his slumped shoulders and unhappy eyes and her motherly heart yearned.

'Come on, son, what you want is a good cuppa and I bet you haven't eaten a thing since this morning.'

He summoned a grin. 'I've worked like stink and done exactly nothing.'

'Trying too hard I expect. I'll get you something to eat and then why don't you go to the pictures?'

The warmth of her smile which showed a set of unbelievably white dentures, the greying hair with the cheap perm which gave it a 'frizz' which was almost like his own mother's and the big, pendulous breasts added up to gentleness and comfort. His own mother's generous love towards humanity. This woman who had so little was ready to give kindness and assurance to a man she didn't know, a man with a dark skin and hair like wool. A man that a sleezy little coffee-bar attendant had called handsome and her boy friend a dirty black. Their backgrounds were much the same. Back streets and little education, but what a world of difference in their outlook.

'I'll go to the pictures if you'll let me take you.'

'It's on.'

It was a long time since Doris had been to the pictures. An occasion to be honoured by her best coat and hat, which seldom saw the light of day. She was over-fat, far from elegant and no beauty, but Jeff felt a deep pride in taking her out. She was a woman with a great heart and had given him the freedom of her poor home with utter trust. He had not yet accustomed himself to the muddle of back streets and had not realised in his round about wanderings that the coffee bar was so near Wessex Row. When they passed it he was surprised but felt no concern.

They saw a rip-roaring Western and they both enjoyed it like a couple of children. Doris's 'Ooh's and 'Ah's' filled Jeff with delight. She had a child's simple enjoyment of an exciting story whether phony or not.

They came out of the cinema among a crowd, but it thinned quickly and they turned down the street with the coffee bar. A group of lads stood outside. There was a sudden whispering which Jeff ignored, although he knew it was directed at him. He took Doris's arm and guided her off the pavement to avoid them. There was a snigger. 'Dirty bastard!' muttered someone.

Doris put her head in the air as if she owned the street and they walked on, conscious that they were being followed. They turned into a narrow alley which Doris said was a short cut. A moment later Jeff realised their mistake, for instantly the young toughs caught up and closed them in. They said nothing but stood and grinned in the dim light of the lamp at the end of the alley. Doris, fighting mad and with all her cockney spirit uppermost, glared.

'Get out of the way, you young monkeys. 'Oo do you think you are?'

'It's the nigger who was making up to my Maisie, all right. Get 'im, boys.'

'Doris, get out, quick!' Jeff's voice was husky with fear for her. But not Doris.

'Not so likely.' Her voice was full of defiance and sheer pluck. The boys came on slowly and Jeff waited, determined not to strike the first blow but longing to punch the nearest in the teeth. Then his fear for Doris tempered his anger with common sense.

'Don't be silly. I'm not looking for trouble and I don't suppose you are if you think about it. I just want to walk the lady home quietly.'

'Lady! That old bag! Is that all you can get hold of, nigger?' And the first blow was struck, catching Jeff on the side of the cheek, but it was not just a fist that hit him. It was steel, wickedly sharp. A weaker man might have been knocked cold, but Jeff shook his big head and waded in, scarcely feeling the blows he struck and received. Then the numbers were too great and he was on the ground and felt a devastating blow to his side and another to his back. Running feet, a shrill whistle and it was all over. A burly figure helped him to his feet and he looked for Doris. She was lying by the wall, quite still. His head was swimming, blood dripped from his cheek and a gash in his forehead and one eye was almost closed, but he was down on his knees beside her, his arm under her neck, cradling the over-permed head against his breast.

'Best not move her, sir, we've sent for the ambulance. Do you know her?'

'She's my landlady. Oh, dear God, that this should happen.'

'We've got three of the lads. You look as if you need a bit of attention yourself.'

At the hospital Doris was wheeled away and a nurse took Jeff into a cubicle. She cleaned up his face and a doctor stitched up the gashes on his forehead and cheek. There were three cracked ribs and a great many bruises. Jeff's thoughts were with Doris and he grew more and more impatient at the time being spent on him.

'It's Doris, Mrs. Burton, how is she?'

'Don't worry, she's being taken care of.' Jeff suddenly realised that the white-coated figure was someone from the islands. Not that it mattered. 'Who is she?'

'Mrs Burton, my landlady. I'd taken her to a picture.'

Then came the questions from the police. A sergeant was now on the spot. He looked at Jeff doubtfully.

'One of the lads we have in custody says you were trying to get hold of his girl. Is there any truth in that?'

'No.' Jeff tried to be patient but he wanted to know about Doris.

'Do you know her?'

'Do you mean Mrs. Burton? Of course I know her. She's my landlady.'

'No, I mean this lad's girl. Do you know her?'

Jeff tried to explain that he had only seen the girl once, earlier that day in a coffee bar and she had smiled and the boy had taken exception to it. To his own ears it did not sound convincing. He could have been making a pass at her. He did not mention the conversation he had heard as he went out of the bar.

'Well, if you were making a pass at her it is no excuse for assault.'

So he was right. The sergeant did think he had been making a pass. Jeff was beyond common sense.

'Go and look at the girl and you'll get your answer. She is hardly my type.' The words and tone were insulting and he knew it.

The sergeant gave him a cold look. 'There is no need to take that attitude. All we want is the truth.'

'And all I want to know is whether Mrs. Burton is badly hurt. She is my responsibility. It wouldn't have happened to her had she not been with me.'

A doctor came in. 'Mrs. Burton is up in the ward. You can see her but she is still unconscious. There's no fracture and when she comes to we hope that all she will need is rest.'

The sergeant went with him and Jeff wondered if he, too, was under arrest. Doris lay in the high, white bed, curtains drawn closely round. There was a nasty bruise on her face and, now the unbelievable teeth had been removed, her mouth sunk in, making her look very old and helpless. Jeff sat by the bed and took the toil-worn hand in his and prayed, silently. Then he looked up at the sergeant, his full, black eyes tear-filled.

'I wanted her to run but she wouldn't. It didn't matter about me but she is old and kind and has been very good to me.'

The sorrow in the rich voice moved the sergeant more than a thousand words could have done.

'She'll be all right. Don't worry. Poor old soul's had a shock and she hit her head when they knocked her down.'

A nurse came and stood by the bed, taking the plump wrist in her hand and looking at her watch.

'What she will need is a few days' rest. You'd better get home to bed yourself.'

The sergeant took him home in a police car. His manner was now more friendly and his questions less official. Jeff, now his anxiety about Doris was eased, returned to his more gentle self and explained quietly what had happened.

'You say you are a reporter and doing an article for the *Meteor*. Have you any objection to us checking with the editor?'

'No, of course not. I wish to the Lord I had already written that article.'

'Take it easy for a couple of days and then get down to it. The area where you are living is hardly the district for a writer, is it.'

'Do you know what it is like to look for lodgings when you have a brown skin? I had nowhere to stay. An old couple called Jones and Mrs. Burton have been good Samaritans.'

'I see. Well, in the short time you have been here you can't say you have been dull, although for our sakes, yours and the old lady's, I wish you had. Here you are and I hope you have a good night's sleep. Don't forget the magistrates' court in the morning.'

It was the last thing Jeff wanted, but it was something that could not be avoided. He could hardly expect the police to let the young hooligans go free just because he didn't want to give evidence.

He made himself a cup of tea and went up to bed, wishing from the bottom of his heart that he could soak in a hot bath and get some of the pain out of his aching body. He looked at his face in the spotty mirror. What a mess! There was a great bag under one eye and his lips were bruised and swollen. What with that and the dressings on his cheek and forehead he was far from a pretty sight. The thought of Maisie calling him 'Handsome' brought a faint and rather rueful smile. If it hadn't been for that damn girl this would never have happened. Make a pass at her! Perish the thought. Repulsive little ghoul!

2

The formal hearing at the magistrates' court was far quicker than he expected. The boys were committed for trial and it was over. When he got back to Wessex Row there was a messenger on the doorstep with a letter from Gordon Robertson asking him to see him at the office. Jeff was news.

'I asked you to come because it was easier and quicker than writing. We'd like three articles from you and this is a firm commission. We won't publish until the trial comes up when they will be given more space. First the one we talked of, secondly one on youngsters here and those back in your own home and a third on the reasons why your people come. God knows you don't get much of a welcome and you've had a really bad one. Deal with them in your own way and if they are not quite what we want I'll help you knock them into shape.'

'I know nothing of your youngsters here. I've only just come and you can hardly call my brush with a few young toughs a knowledge of what the average youngster is like.'

'By the look of your face it was more than a brush!' Robertson grinned. 'You're a writer. It's up to you to find out. As these are commissioned articles we will give you a retaining fee now if you agree not to write for any other paper until after they are published.'

The sum Robertson offered was too good to refuse. It was towards the passage of Lucy and the children, towards establishing a home. It was a very thoughtful Jeff who was driven back to Wessex Row.

When he went to see Doris she had not only recovered consciousness but was very much on the upward trend. Her dentures were in and her cockney spirit uppermost.

'Fat lot of good I was!' She was indignant. 'Just as I was going to 'it one of them over the 'ead with my bag another one knocked me down and I don't know nothink after that. Coo, you do look a mess! All I got was a bump on me 'ead and this bruise on me face. Not even a shiner. My Reggie won't 'alf be mad when 'e comes out. Got 'is faults but 'e wouldn't do nothink like that.'

She didn't seem to notice she had given her Reggie's whereabouts away.

'The doctor won't let me out yet so you'll 'ave to look after yerself fer a bit, son.'

'That's all right, Doris, you just get fit and the rest will do you good.'

She gave a hoarse chuckle. 'First time I've 'ad a rest since my Reggie was born. Waited on 'and and foot I am and I'm going to make the most of it.'

'You do just that.'

Jeff wandered around London. To him it seemed never

35

ending. Backstreet slums; little old cottages that looked as if they belonged in the country; great blocks of grey, dirty flats put up before anyone thought of comfort or even reasonable hygiene. It was unbelievable. Beautiful buildings, hideous ones. They jostled each other astonishingly. Lovely houses lying back from the roads with well-tended gardens, street after street of middle-class dwellings. Shops of any and every kind. People swarming the pavements as if they had nothing else to do but walk and stare. Others rushing as if they hadn't a moment to live. White faces, black faces, yellow faces. Transport crowding the roads until traffic came to a standstill. Transport of every kind. Buses, cycles, motor-bikes, cars of every description and in the city he saw a brewers dray drawn by two enormous white horses. A city of amazing contrasts in which anything could happen and often did. It was a vast jungle of buildings and people. Nothing he had read could have prepared him.

At last the articles were finished. He took them to Robertson who blue pencilled and wrote in until Jeff wondered what would be left of his own efforts.

'You can write but not pungent enough.' Robertson gave one of his rare smiles. 'On the other hand we don't want it too biting. Just a bit of spice.'

The cheque went straight into the bank. He had enough to live on till his next article was sold which he was convinced would be soon.

Doris came home and then there was the trial. Bert Foster got six months but partly because of his truculence. He didn't need anyone to help him 'do' that dirty nigger who had tried to get hold of his girl. Unfortunately for him Maisie had got the sack from her job and disappeared into the jungle that was London. Robertson came forward with glee to testify that it was most unlikely for a man who

36

was an eminent writer (Jeff gave a slight smile at this) in own country to make up to a girl who had been given the sack for causing trouble and was known to be free with her favours. At which Foster let out a string of oaths that did not improve his case. When it was over Jeff breathed a sigh of relief. He could now get on with his life.

Slowly his high hopes vanished. The *Meteor* took no more articles. Robertson would have liked to, but Jeff was no longer news and he wrote nothing suitable, although his work was fair. He haunted the library until the assistants began to think he was becoming a fixture. He sent articles to paper after paper, to magazine after magazine, but, apart from two short ones to provincials, they all came back with rejection slips. He had little knowledge of what editors needed and there seemed no way of finding out. His money was vanishing even more quickly than his hopes. He remembered Robertson's words: 'Take any ruddy job you can get and write in your spare time.'

The job-hunting period began. The fact that he was a writer was no help at all, for he had no other qualifications. He had interview after interview and they got him no-where. It was plain that clerical jobs were out.

Politeness nearly everywhere, but there was always an excuse and he was down to his last few pounds. Fear that he would have to dip into the money he had received from the *Meteor* spurred him on even when he felt it was useless to look any more. He began to think of labouring. He made no friends apart from the three old people who had been his refuge. And then Reg came home. Reg, a long, thin thirty with mousy hair, a long nose and blackened teeth, but with hands that could have been a poet's joy. He was nothing that Jeff had expected and was completely unabashed by his spells in prison and Jeff wondered why Doris made such an effort to cover up for him. Reg listened to Doris's racy account of the attack on Jeff, the little she knew of it, and he made a few very crisp comments and grinned at Jeff.

'My old mum's a one!' He put an arm round her fat shoulders and grinned and there was pride and affection in his voice. What was even more astonishing was that he spoke far better than could have been expected and he announced that he intended to go straight in future. Jeff, having heard of his escapades from Alf, wondered if it would last, but he could not help liking the man. The biggest problem was finding somewhere for Jeff, but Reggie solved it. As Jeff worked in the front room they could borrow a camp-bed until he found somewhere. Through the prisoners' aid he had already a job to go to and was concerned that Jeff was still hunting for one. But Reg was the born solver of other people's problems even if he wasn't always able to solve his own.

'You're barking up the wrong tree. You don't want to try a private office. Some employers are afraid to employ a coloured man in case a lot of his people walk out on him. They may be afraid you've enough brains to move up before they do and that wouldn't be nice, would it? Then there are the others who are dead scared a nigger would rape one of the girls on or under the desk. Black men are supposed to be much more virile and far less controlled when it comes to sex than a white man.'

The grin took the sting out of the words and for the first time Jeff heard the word 'nigger' without recoil and even with some amusement. Reggie was stating facts and not being insulting. The way he said the word made it clear he was using it not as his own but as he had heard it used by others.

'Then there are some white men who are scared because they think women might be attracted. Colour doesn't make

38

much difference when a man's good-looking and got a nice way and you're too good-looking for your own good. Now take me. No bloke is ever afraid I'll pinch his girl. Women never look at me twice.'

'Then what do you suggest?'

'Try London Transport. They want booking-office clerks. Think of all the free travel!'

At London Transport people were pleasant. Once or twice he heard complaints about too many immigrants and very occasionally he heard worse, but he refused to let it worry him. He was growing a veneer, a hard crust which let nothing penetrate. And the need for Lucy was growing less. He and Reggie became close in a way he wouldn't have thought possible. He sold three more short articles to provincials, but that was all. The others were returned with only rejection slips and he lost heart. What was the use of writing if it was not accepted? He didn't tell Lucy, for fear it worried her and that made his letters stilted, shorter and less frequent. Hers remained the same, loving, giving the latest news of the children, but, after a time, they, too, became less frequent, although she never complained. She had always been the accepting kind. Sometimes he would close his eyes and try to picture her face, but it eluded him and only by getting out her photo could he see her sweet expression and rounded body. The only thing that remained vivid was in the night when he felt the soft fulness of her breasts and the warmth and comfort of her hands and arms around him, but in the morning there was no memory left.

At times he was tempted to try to contact some of his own people, but he couldn't bring himself to acknowledge that Jeff Anderson was now a booking clerk on London Transport. It was silly pride and he knew it and that made him even more ashamed. Often he yearned for a long chat with some of his old friends whom he knew were in England, but it was George he thought of more than anyone. George, the skinny, barefoot boy his father had encouraged and coached at every available moment. The boy who had passed one exam after another until he finally got his scholarship to medical school. The plain, near-sighted boy for whom he had always felt a deep attraction and yet the feeling had been a strange mixture. A sort of love-hate relationship. Pity for the boy's physical inability to cope with the bullying element in some of the bigger boys, pride in fighting his battles for him in the earlier years, jealousy for his tenacity and mental capacity which seemed to have no limit. And Jeff loved him because it was his nature to love the weak and helpless and he hardly realised that, over the years, George had conquered his physical weakness in much the same way as he had conquered his studies, with a determination which was not ruthless but purposeful. He hadn't grown a fine physique, nature had denied him that, but he had developed his muscles and the bigger boys no longer bullied him.

It wasn't until Jeff and Lucy were engaged that the friendship had at last dwindled and Jeff accepted it as one of the things that was bound to happen as you matured. Occasionally they would have an evening together, but George had altered. He was no longer the little boy looking up to his protector. He tried to spur Jeff on, he was critical, he wanted to know when the book was going to be written. There would be an amiable grin from Jeff.

'You're in such a flaming hurry, George. A book needs time and I'm working pretty hard.'

'But the book isn't even started! You could spend less time at the club, less time dreaming of what you are going to do.'

'And become so dull I wouldn't be able to write at all.'

'Maybe you're right and I've become a complete bore.'

That was years ago and the book still wasn't started. The last time he had heard of George he was working in a hospital in Birmingham. Now, as he walked wet pavements under grey skies, his thoughts turned more often than he liked to George. How right he had been. If only he had applied himself as George had done, worked with that same purpose to get a degree or write a book, he might have something at the back of him now. Instead of which he had lingered on sandy beaches, gone dancing and picnicking with his friends, enjoyed thinking of what he would do rather than doing it. Life had been altogether too easy and now he was paying for it.

Spring came and the daffodils bloomed in the parks, trees put forth tender green leaves, and Jeff, seeing the delicate beauty that draped grey old London, ached with longing for the smell of frangipani and the sight of flaming canna lilies and walls hung with purple and red bougainvillaea. He had been eight months in England and all he had to show for it was the money for those first three articles. Time was slipping by relentlessly.

Just as he had almost given up hope of finding a place on his own Reg came up with the news that there was a flatlet to let in Lenning Road.

'It'll cost you more but you'll have room to move and the beds are good. There's a bathroom on the lower floor!' Reg grinned, knowing the frequent visits Jeff payed to the public baths. 'Constant hot water, too.'

Mrs. Morris wasn't interested in his colour, she wasn't interested in her tenants as people at all. All she asked was that they paid their rent and behaved themselves. The house had been left to her by an aunt and late in life she had married an ex-boxer, good-looking in a big, blond way, years younger than herself and fond of a drink. Not that he ever got drunk, just enough to make him occasionally slip over the traces, but he did his bit in the house, painting and cleaning with a bit of plumbing thrown in for good measure. Strangely enough, he hadn't married her for what he could get out of her but had genuinely been attracted by her higher education, business brain and lady-like manners. He was extremely fond of her and they got on remarkably well in spite of their differences in temperament, background and everything else. The funniest thing was that big Bill Morris was scared sick of his small wife, although she treated him like an overgrown schoolboy.

Jeff's room was an attic at the back. It was light and bright and the dormer window looked out over a maze of roofs. Perhaps here he would get down to writing and it wasn't too far from Reggie and the others. But here his loneliness was more marked and slowly he realised he was nothing like the man who had left the island—or had he ever been the man he thought he was? Back home he had been a good and loving son, husband and father—or he thought he had. He had worked hard, played hard and slept hard. If not a complete extrovert at least he had plenty of friends and enjoyed their company. He had liked and admired women, but now there were times when he hated them. Back home they had been a source of pleasure, but there was always Lucy and he was not a highly sexed man. Lucy had satisfied all of his physical needs and a great many of his spiritual and mental. She was gentle and loving and accepted him as he was without expecting too much. It was as simple as that. Now, in London Transport, he met a lot of women, black, white and all the colours in between.

There was the pretty, slim, coffee-coloured porter with the roving eye and eager smile. There was the redhead with light grey eyes which held a definite invitation and the bouncing woman from Barbados with hips that swung provocatively. She was the one who drove him right into his shell and earned him the character of 'bighead' among the women, although luckily he got on with the men. Her name was Althea and her eyes were loving and whenever opportunity arose she would have coffee or tea with Jeff. Her undoing came when she asked him to go to a dance. Perhaps, had he gone, it might have ended differently, for she brought him a smell of the islands, the sound of the sea on moonlit nights and the throb of steel bands. A dance, no, he might meet someone he knew and if he did how would he explain the presence of a woman with him? Non-conformist principles had been sucked in with his mother's milk.

She replied that she was not keen herself, so why not come home and have a meal—a real West Indian meal—and then watch television? He knew she had a schoolgirl daughter so it was just a friendly invitation and the temptation was too much.

The schoolgirl daughter was staying the night with friends, which was something the warm and friendly Althea had not mentioned. The meal was excellent and afterwards she turned on television which was her joy and her delight. The flat was comfortable and she proudly told him the furniture was her own. She had been in England six years and actually liked it. If there was or had been a husband she didn't mention him.

'You know,' she said, conversationally, ignoring the programme on the square box utterly, 'a place never seems right without a man. Now seeing you sitting there makes it home.'

Jeff was lost for words and found the situation getting out of hand. In the dim light from the one small lamp she looked very attractive. Her brown skin was smooth and unlined, her black hair drawn into a fashionable swathe at the back and her neat legs stretched out in front of her.

'Downright silly for two people to keep two flats when one is enough. Much cheaper living together. I wouldn't say this to any man but I feel on my own since my friend's wife came over. He's got money and bought this house. That's how I got the flat. He's moved away with his wife and baby and Jean and I have been on our own ever since.'

Jeff panicked like a schoolboy and said he had to be going. It wasn't until he was walking vigorously that he knew why he had panicked. He hated his present life, he missed the comforts of home, and suddenly sex was there, mocking him, making him long for a woman's arms with an ache that was maddeningly persistent. He walked the five miles back and when he arrived at his flatlet he flung himself on his bed and hid his face in his folded arms. What was happening to him in this Godless city?

After that he nodded politely to any of the women, avoiding even a pleasant conversation and he turned inwards more and more. He wrote to Lucy more frequently and tried to recapture the earlier tenderness he had poured out, but words of any kind now eluded him. He had no ideas, no ability whatsoever, and he sunk deeper and deeper into a rut of his own making. He could have gone to church, but he no longer felt any leaning towards it, and yet somewhere, deep down, he longed for the faith of his parents and his own childhood. And clear memories of Lucy still eluded him. He saw less and less of the three old people and Reggie and when he did go for a drink with him Reggie, too, seemed to have altered.

The reason for that came out one evening.

'I've got the chance of a job in one of the new towns outside of London. A new flat and more money.'

44

'I'll miss you, Reg, but it's a good opportunity.'

'It would be if I could persuade my old girl to move. Cussed old devil. She says she'd have to give up her job and that she won't do. Been independent all her life and is going on the same until she has to give up. Imagine, turning down the chance of a modern flat for a dump like the place in Wessex Row which is due for demolition anyhow. I could get a secondhand car and bring her to see her pals sometimes and she's a matey sort and would soon make friends. Besides, I want to get away. Know too many people round here and they're only waiting for me to step out of the straight and narrow so they can say it is just what they expected. I'm doing well at the factory.' He stretched out his delicate hand. 'Got the right hands for tricky jobs.'

'Can't you talk her round?'

'Not on your sweet life.' Reg downed his beer in a gulp. 'Makes me mad. Just as I've got the chance to make things easier for her. I've been a lousy son until now, I know, but she won't give me the chance to make things better. You know, Jeff, it was that damned business with the boys that helped me to go straight. The thought of her being in that hospital while I was in clink brought me up with a round turn.'

'Reg, let me have a talk to her and you take the job before you lose the chance. She'll go with you.'

Jeff was off the following morning and went to see Doris before she left for her cleaning job. She greeted him with delight and announced that there was time for a cuppa before she went. Jeff sat down and watched her bustling around, her fat figure shaking like a jelly.

'You know, Doris, I always thought you were a wonderful mother.'

She poured out the tea and looked at him. 'And now

you've changed your mind.' Her tones were slightly ag-
gressive. 'I suppose my Reggie's been talking about that
job.'

'Yes, he has and I'm ashamed of you. He's got the chance
to get away from all the things and people who made him
what he was. He's doing well and you're not helping him
much, are you?'

'I've lived in this place ever since I was married.'

'Time you had a change! You did the best you could for
Reggie. You always stood by him whatever happened,
but now you're being selfish and won't let him do what he
can for you. Denying him the chance of making up for
the past.'

'And suppose 'e wants to get married? What 'appens
then?'

'That's a chance you'll have to take.'

Two big tears rolled down the fat cheeks. 'I don't know
what to do.'

'Go with him all the way and risk the future. Let him be
the son he wants to be. Suppose he never meets a girl he
wants to marry? You make a home for him where he wants.
I'll tell you this, he won't go without you and who's to
know, if he stays here, he won't slip back into his old ways
at sometime?'

Jeff didn't think for a moment he would, but his words
worked and Reggie and Doris moved to the new town.
When they had gone Jeff felt that a part of him had gone
with them.

Summer had come and gone. Some days the sun was
bright and the mild warmth seeped into his soul and the
memory of white sands and sparkling seas was a knife in
his heart. It was almost as if the island itself meant more
to him than its people. He welcomed the grey days of
autumn which wiped out memory. He was trying to save

money but it wasn't easy. He had been in England over a year and he needed more clothes. His shirts were fraying at the cuffs and collars, his socks were wearing out and his underclothes getting ragged. Laundries were expensive and wore them out far quicker than at home. The idea of washing them himself had never occurred to him.

His letters now said nothing of Lucy and the children joining him, but Lucy seemed perfectly happy. She was enjoying teaching again, the children were growing at a terrible rate and the house was still let. The English couple were leaving soon, but she knew she could let it to Americans and they would pay more. It seemed that he was no longer needed. Why bother to try to save money? Why not enjoy himself? He bought presents for Christmas and sent them off. He also bought presents for Liz and Alf, Doris and Reg.

Reg and Doris insisted that he should spend Christmas with them. Reg now had his car and he was fetching Liz and Alf for the day. Jeff went with them. Boxing Day he was on duty.

It was a quiet day, mostly spent watching 'telly', eating an enormous meal somewhere about three o'clock in the afternoon and being driven home by an ecstatic Reg in the early hours of the morning. Reg had found himself. Whether he would ever get married was another matter. He was convinced no woman would look at him twice and it didn't appear to worry him. He was helping to run a youth club in the new town, was perfectly honest with everyone about his past and doing his utmost to be a good citizen. Doris had settled down as if it had been her home for years.

'Wish you'd come out there, Jeff. I could get you a job. You might do a bit of writing for our firm's magazine. It's not bad, either. Are you writing at all?'

47

Jeff shook his head. 'No time.'

'If you were with us you'd have more time. The old lady would love to have you and we've got the room.' He grinned. 'Think of our lovely new bathroom and all the beautiful hot water!'

'I'll think about it, Reg.'

But he knew he wouldn't, although he had no idea why, unless it was because while he was in London he still had the elusion that Fleet Street was round the corner and at some time he would get in.

But the day with Reg and Doris had made his loneliness more acute. He must do something other than work, sleep and eat, or his brain would atrophy. Evening classes could have been the answer, but shift work put that right out. He had time to write and knew it but he kept putting it off. Then he found an outlet for part of his mind at least. He began to haunt museums and art galleries much as at one time he had haunted the library. Loneliness was something he must learn to accept while he did his best to enjoy the richness that was London. Yet underneath this effort at self-negation was a resentment at his loneliness. A growing misery that ate into his vitals.

It was the last day in January and he had the day off. He spent most of it at the Victoria and Albert Museum, drinking in the loveliness of old things, of delicate craftmanship and glowing colour, making his loneliness bite deeper, feeling the ineffectuality of his life cut into him like a knife. Longing to do something but utterly incapable of putting his longing into a force for work. It was so much simpler to drift with the tide. Back home it had carried him along on a gentle current. He had never had to struggle against it and now it did not seem as if he would ever find the incentive to try. Lucy was managing without his help, so why bother? He had a sinking in the pit of his stomach.

It wasn't like being a man at all. He was just a thing, a robot, without real emotion or brain, with nothing left but to work, to eat and to sleep.

He had a meal in the cafeteria because that would save him bothering about more than bread and cheese when he got in. He was caring less and less about what he ate or when. On the way home he was suddenly and inexplicably extravagant. He bought an electric percolator. Until now he had been making tea or instant coffee because it was easier. Now he would make real coffee, coffee in the morning. It was a warming thought and made him feel less of an automaton.

Way back in the West Indies he had parents, a wife and children, but now he was a man on his own—a bachelor. It was a cold, grey day and nearly dark. A coloured girl went into the Tube station ahead of him wearing a bright red coat and a pert white hat. She glanced over her shoulder. Neat features, slim legs. It would be good to take a girl out for once. Someone to talk to, to smile at, to laugh with. He wasn't thinking of Lucy at all. There was no longing for her in particular. Just the company of a woman. He wasn't even conscious of sex desire. Just the need to be with a woman.

A smartly dressed lad came towards the girl and took her briefly in his arms. Lucky bastard! Better not think about it. Tonight he would definitely get down to some writing. What about? An article on how London could grow on a stranger? And how did he think he was going to sell it and where? If he didn't write it he wouldn't know! He had let things slide and Lucy and the children down. Time he pulled himself together and did something about it. Perhaps now he had had experience he could get a better job. Perhaps he would again approach Gordon Robertson. West Indians in England! Good Lord, he knew nothing about them—nor the English for that matter!

He washed the percolator carefully and put the coffee in the container. As it began to bubble the rich, pungent smell assailed his nostrils and made the silence of the room more acute, wakening him to the bitterness of near defeat.

Oh, snap out of it! Enjoy what he had, new sights, new scenes and, at this moment, good, strong coffee, scalding hot, biting bitter.

He was just going to put the milk on to heat when he remembered it was still in the hall. He ran down the stairs thinking of nothing but rich, strong, coffee.

3

The bleary-eyed old man leered up at the girl. His loose-lipped mouth was parted in a grin, showing broken-down brown teeth with hideous gaps in between, his tongue hung, pink, salivarously repulsive behind them. He put out a filthy hand and touched her smooth, brown arm.

She said nothing but her eyes were murderous and she gave a vicious flick at his dirty paw with the wet cloth she had been using on the table. He glared back at her.

'Nasty-tempered little bitches, you niggers,' he muttered.

She swung away from the table, her head high, her thin legs moving rhythmically. Stopping to gather up the dirty crockery at the next table she scarcely saw the two leather-jacketed, long-haired boys until one of them spoke.

'You can't blame the old bastard for trying.' It was a good-looking face, strong, white teeth, firm lips and clear skin, but the look in the eyes was lascivious. It was as much as she could do to keep the wet cloth from the smiling face, but she said nothing. She'd got to keep this job, got to, for a few weeks at least. She had been in and out of too many since she came to England and there was very little money left. Some of them she had lost through her own fault, she knew that, none better. Some of them because some filthy Englishman thought she was fair game. She had come to hate their white skins with a murderous bitterness, just as she hated the women, but she wasn't quite sure why she hated them. Perhaps because some of them were kind, too kind, with a condescension which jarred like a slap in the face. It was easier to accept insults. She went on wiping tables spitefully, her hate showing in every movement, her full mouth, which could have been passionately loving, set in a tight line.

'I'm sorry.' The middle-aged man looked at her sadly. The voice was cultured, he was shabby but clean and the light blue eyes were worried. 'It's just ignorance, you know.'

'And you'd like to show this poor nigger girl how kind white men can be!' Her voice was low but her words carried to the two boys and there was a yell of laughter.

The middle-aged man's pale cheeks flushed and he buttered the roll in front of him with as much concentration as he could muster and again muttered, 'I'm sorry!'

She knew her words had been unforgivable, she knew it was not condescension which had prompted his words but sheer kindness. But why should she care? She hated England, she hated the English, and perhaps, more than anything, she hated herself.

Jack, the big, blond owner of the café, eyed her resentfully. It was difficult to get help, but he couldn't afford to employ a girl who gave the customers lip. Start off an argument before you could look round and then there could be a rough house. She was a damn pretty girl and could be an asset, but if she was going to chew customers up and spit them out it wouldn't do. It didn't matter about old Joe, he was a damn nuisance anyhow. Spent hours on one cup of tea, but the teenagers spent money these days and he wasn't going to have them upset. Now Rosie could handle them. Whatever they said she gave them a cheeky grin and a flick of her skirts and Bob's your uncle. He'd better speak to Anne. There was a rush of customers and it was midnight before he got the chance to say anything.

'Look, girl, if you want to keep this job you'd better treat the customers decently.'

'Then you'd better tell them to treat me the same.' Her dark brown eyes were sullen.

'If you mean old Joe I'll tell him any time. He's a damn nuisance and the sooner he finds somewhere else to plant himself the better.'

Jack closed the door and pulled down the blinds. Rosie was clearing the last of the dirty crockery from the tables and William, the boy from Granada, was washing up in the kitchen.

Anne stood quite still, her hands clenched by her sides.

'You don't do so badly here.' Jack turned to face her. 'You pick up a bit in tips. By all accounts you've been in one job after another since you came over. You want to treat the customers like Rosie does. She gives them a laugh and a joke and they leave her alone.'

'Oh, come orf it, Jack. Anne'll be all right when she gets used to it. Too late to start nattering now. Can't it wait till the morning. Come on, Anne, it's late.'

Jack shook his head. It wasn't any good trying to say anything with Rosie about. Her pert grin disarmed him as it did everyone else. The two girls went off towards the

High Street, their high heels clicking on the pavement.

'You don't want to take no—any notice.' Rosie's chirruping, cockney voice lost none of its gaiety in spite of the fact that she was dead tired. 'Be a bit bright and stick it out till you've got something better, that's my motto. You don't think I'm going to stay there any longer than I can 'elp, do yer?' They stopped at the kerb to let a car pass. 'I'm going to better myself. Saving all I can so I can get a room on my own and I'm going to get a job in a place up west. I've got a boy friend who's been to grammar school. Not serious, just a bit of fun, but he speaks nice and I'm going to learn.' Anne didn't speak and Rosie giggled. 'Not going to tie myself to anyone, kid, not till I've 'ad some fun and moved up a bit. Not going to be like me mum. Nine kids and not even a bathroom! But there, I suppose you're used to that sort of thing.'

'Yes.' Anne spoke at last and there was bitterness in her voice, but underlying it was amusement. Rosie was not yet eighteen, but she was nobody's fool, and there was something about Anne that touched her warm, cockney heart. 'Just a shanty down on the beach and ten children. All I wore until I was grown up was a cotton frock. But the weather was warm and we could always sleep on the beach when a baby was being born.' She paused to let that sink in, a devil inside enjoying Rosie's sympathy while she was laughing at her expense, unaware that Rosie was too shrewd to believe the lot. 'We weren't really hungry because there's lots of fruit. When I was twelve I went to work for a white woman. She was a devil. That's why I came to England as soon as I could. I thought it would be better here.'

'Tell you what,' Rosie said, 'when we get a Saturday night off together you come dancing with me and my boy friend. He'd bring a friend.'

'Thank you, Rosie, perhaps I will. Good night.' She turned off down her own tatty street, hoping Rosie didn't see how her shoulders were shaking, or if she did that she would think she was crying for the awful past. It was the first good laugh she had had in months.

Rose was wondering why Anne had exaggerated quite so much, for she was perfectly sure she had never left school at twelve, although she could have been very poor. Poor thing, was it because she needed sympathy so much? Rosie was more sorry for her than ever.

Anne opened the front door and went up the lino-covered stairs, carefully avoiding the one that creaked, curling her nose fastidiously at the smell of stale cooking and musty dampness which seemed to cling to every bit of the dirty walls and send it back at her in nauseating waves. Her door creaked protestingly and she switched on the hard, white light and stared round the small room with distaste. Smuts from the open window had sprinkled the cheap cover on the bed, but if she closed it to keep them out the room would smell just as sickly as the rest of the house. Dear Lord, what wouldn't she give for a shower to wash away the sweat which made her feel so disgustingly unclean. She slipped off her shoes and put the kettle on the gas ring, moving silently in stockinged feet. She couldn't sleep until she had washed off the day's grime.

The stuffiness of the room, the sordid furniture, the creaking bed, drove away sleep and then she remembered Rosie and again shook with silent laughter. What an ignorant fool the girl was. A shanty on the beach and ten children! She had taken it all in. Her contempt for English ignorance was the one thing left which had the power to make her laugh. The one thing which saved her from utter self-loathing. She put her folded arms behind her head to protect it from the lumpy pillow and stretched out her long, thin legs. What would her father say if he knew what she had come to? No doubt tell her it was her own fault but send her the money to go home. Go home to be treated like a stupid child by Lydia! She'd die first.

Her lips curled up at the memory of Rosie. Rosie, with her pert, pretty face, the honey-gold eyes and that golden-red hair piled high on her head. Rosie with that gorgeous figure and her knack of handling men, which, Anne thought, was about all she did know apart from her speed at serving customers.

How horrified her father would be if he knew what she had told Rosie. She thought of the smart house on the outskirts of town, the two cars, the two maids and the pretty garden. Her stepmother's beautiful clothes, the bridge parties and the dinners. She refused to think of her two little half-brothers because they were the ones she missed. Her father had been so coldly angry when she refused to accept her stepmother as her own, but she had been only eleven at the time and her own mother so fresh in her memory. Lydia was everything her own mother was not. Young, pretty and gay, and what made it worse was that her older brother and sister adored her. Well, she hated her. But she couldn't hate little Colin and Michael. She wanted to, but against her will they had conquered her. When she failed her G.C.E. her father had been furious. He wanted her to get degrees the same as her brother and sister had done, but she didn't care. She had been pleased to fail him and refused to try again. She had taken job after job and didn't like any of them and when she was nineteen had calmly informed them she was coming to England. She was certain in her heart her father had breathed a sigh of relief. The problem child was leaving. He had paid her fare, given her money and written to her cousin Claudia, who was married and living in Cardiff. Claudia was a nurse and had married a doctor from Trinidad.

She had taken a job in a shop, although both Claudia and Robert had said it would be much better to study. Anne had no intention of being co-operative. No, London was the place.

She had never written to Claudia since she left Cardiff, nor to her family at home. As far as she was concerned they could all go to the devil—except little Colin and Michael. Well, they didn't know what she had come to and they were not likely to and nothing would make her go back. Go back and admit she had been a fool! Not likely. Put up with and laugh at the stupid English but never give in. Live like a pig in a sty but never give in.

She turned restlessly and the bed creaked. The room was unbearably stuffy. She got up and opened the window at the bottom and leant out. A goods train chugged and bumped over the points. A smell of garbage came up from the yard. Suddenly she longed for the sound of waves on a sandy beach and the sough of the wind in the trees and the clean, sweet smell. Silly Rose, what did she think she could do with her life? Better herself! Why, she was just as much a prisoner of circumstance as she was herself. The only difference was that she had a white skin and it made it easier. Her boy friend who had been to grammar school! Anne tried to picture him. A boy with a slight veneer of culture trying to be what he was not, trying to move up in the social scale, looking down on Rosie but accepting her gaiety and fun. Strangely, that thought annoyed her. Rosie might be a fool, but she was good-hearted. Rosie's complete ignorance of anything to do with the West Indies amused her, but also made her contemptuous. She had never realised how ignorant the English were, forgetting the number of West Indians who had arrived in

England equally ignorant of the land they thought of as full of promise.

She moved her arms from the sill, realising with disgust that they were now covered with soot. Washing them once more, she lay down on the bed and, suddenly, with the resilience of youth, she was asleep.

During the next two or three weeks she managed to curb her turbulent temper. May gave way to June with a burst of heat that was stifling and unexpected. Anne didn't know which was worse, the heat or the cold, and had she not needed the money would have thrown up the job. But however much she hated it she still had to eat and have somewhere to sleep. She did her utmost not to see the eyes that looked at her, whether with admiration or lust. She accepted Rosie's friendship with amusement and because there was nobody else. She dare not mix with West Indians in case she should meet with someone who would know her and write to her father. What she was going to do with her life she had no idea. For the present it was a matter of keeping alive.

One Saturday she went to a dance with Rosie because anything was better than going back to the stale-smelling, dirty little room. The dance hall was hot and stuffy and the smell of tight-packed humanity, not always as clean as it should be, roused even more contempt and hatred. Rosie's boy friend was not what she expected. He spoke well, was quietly dressed and he clearly admired Rosie a great deal. His friend, Ted, was older, more experienced. He spoke well, danced well, his clothes were well cut and he was completely adult. He looked at Anne carefully and weighed her up with shrewd eyes.

'What made you come?' he asked.

'I might ask the same question. I shouldn't think this is your usual haunt and you're a good bit older than Jim.'

'If you must know it is because I'm fond of Jim. I know his people and I wanted to meet Rosie.'

'And you would like to break it up because you don't think she is good enough for him!'

'Well, well, well!' He chuckled. 'Rosie has a champion in an unexpected quarter. From you that is funny, seeing that you told her such a lot of rubbish.'

'What are you talking about?' There was biting anger in her voice, the continual anger which was becoming part of her. In the café she was learning to cover it, but here there was no need. Nobody was going to make fun of her whatever she did to other people.

'Rosie, bless her kind heart, has talked to Jim about you. He's a hard-working youngster who is going to make good. Willing to start at the bottom as a motor mechanic so that he can become a car salesman and know what he is talking about. Whether he and Rosie will end up going steady I wouldn't know, but if they do she won't let him down. She's a jolly nice girl. She wasn't a bit of a surprise. Jim has never tried to paint her as anything other than what she is. You are the surprise. You've tried to fill her up with a pretty tissue of lies, haven't you, and whether it was to make game of her or get pity I wouldn't know, although I expect it was just sheer unkindness. You've got a real chip on your shoulder, haven't you, and a nasty streak beside.'

Anne stared at him, her mouth set in a hard line and her eyes furious. Ted Robson grinned.

'You'd like to spit in my eye, wouldn't you? Are you really so silly that you think everyone with a white skin is a fool? Rosie was quite aware that you were pulling her leg but she didn't know how much. Knowing you were telling the tale made her even more sorry for you. To her kind heart you must be terribly unhappy. As for me, I happen to know a number of West Indians from the man who cleans the garage to a very eminent doctor. You, my sweet child, come from an upper middle-class family and are probably the misfit. You'd have a chip on your shoulder wherever you were just because life has not worked out exactly as you want it.'

'Damn clever, aren't you? I suppose you think you know all the answers.'

'Not all of them. I just want you to know that you can't fool people just as much as you think. Why don't you go back home and admit you've been a fool or try to fit in here a little more sensibly?'

Her whole body seethed with hate because he had summed her up so neatly.

'You're a pretty girl who could make something of her life instead of wasting it in anger.'

It was made worse by the fact that there was just irritation in his voice for a girl he obviously thought a fool. He wasn't interested in her and she doubted if he even thought about the colour of her skin. Her hatred had nothing to feed on, so it fed on itself, eating her up. She might have liked him a little if she could have felt a slight contempt for his stupidity, but this man was not stupid. There was common sense and knowledge which made her feel a fool. The sense of being beaten roused the devil in her.

'O.K.' She smiled, fitting her steps to his more easily. 'I've been a great big idiot. I left home because I was fed-up. I didn't have any reason apart from the fact that I wouldn't study and I've drifted from one job to another until I'm a waitress in a sleazy coffee bar, so what am I going to do about it? You tell me.' She didn't mention Lydia, knowing instinctively that Ted would approve of that even less than he would stupidity. Pretend to be frank but keep that back.

'Stick the present job until you have proved that you can and then look for something better and do the same again. And stop trying to fool Rosie. She's got a kind heart but she's not dim and she's trying to get out of the rut which her people are in and she'll do it, too.'

For the rest of the evening Anne was thoughtful. Ted was looking at her, his grey eyes twinkling. All right, she'd pay him back in his own coin. If he thought he was smart she could outsmart him. When he asked if she would have a meal with him on her next evening off she hesitated, as if doubtful, and finally said yes.

Being friendly with Ted became a private amusement. Sometimes he took her to quiet, unpretentious restaurants where the food was good, sometimes to the cinema. She didn't talk about home or her people but she did talk of 'Jack's Caff', bringing a pungent sense of humour to play and not realising Ted's shrewd assessment of her feelings. Their outings were never regular for his business took him out of London a good deal but she knew his interest was growing.

In October Rosie got another job. She was mastering her aitches much better now and suddenly burnt her boats.

'I've got a job as mother's help with a nice family. It's the only way to get away from home and live nicely. There's two little kids and the lady's going to have another. I'll have a nice room of my own and there's two bathrooms. Ted Robson got it for me. He knows I'm not afraid of work and it won't be as hard as this. It's the room I really want and I like kids.'

'And you think that bettering yourself?' Anne stared at her.

' 'Course it is. Learn to live nicely and eat decent meals. Bath every day, too.' Rosie gave her pert grin. 'It wouldn't be a bad idea if you got the same sort of job. Damn sight better than living in the poky little room you've got and wondering how to slap the dirty old men down, to say nothing of the fast boys. Jim's ever so pleased.'

'Pleased you're going to be a servant!' The contempt in her voice bit into Rosie's usual good temper.

'All right, I'm going to be a servant, but being a servant ain't what it used to be. It's good pay and easy hours now and I'm going to make a good job of it. I can't see what you've got to be so high and mighty about if what you say about how you were brought up is true.' The honey-gold eyes looked into Anne's thoughtfully. 'Proper fool you must have thought me.' The smile that was never far from Rosie's lips broke through. 'Oh, it don't matter. I never did learn much at school. Stayed away too much to mind the kids, but I didn't believe all the yarns you told. It wasn't because I know anything about the West Indies, either. It was just that I could tell you'd been brought up better than you said. But I do like you, Anne, and I wished you'd get another job. Don't like leaving you here without me. I may be green in some ways but I got me weather eye open in others.'

It hit Anne suddenly that she was going to miss Rosie. Even if she was ignorant in some ways she was wise in others. Apart from that she knew that Rosie had stood between her and Jack's ire on many occasions and often she moved quickly to her rescue when customers were difficult.

'I'll miss you, Rosie.' And Rosie didn't know what a great effort it was for her to admit it. To be warm and friendly was so much part of Rosie's nature that she thought Anne felt the same.

'I'll get my times off and we can go to the pictures, although I'll have to go and see Mum and Dad and the kids sometimes.'

'I'll look for another job, Rosie. Give me your address and we'll keep in touch.'

It was more simple than even Anne had thought. Ted knew of a dentist who wanted a receptionist. He didn't ask for any qualifications. All he wanted was someone who could speak well, write a legible hand and be accurate. Ted was being useful! It was a long way from the poky little room and although the money was far better, travelling expenses were high. Again Ted came to her rescue. He knew of a young couple who wanted to let a room. They were standing at a high mortgage and needed the money. This time there was no walking from door to door as she had when she first came to London. Being turned down with all kinds of excuses which she knew meant, 'We don't like the colour of your skin.'

Anne moved in. The room was small and sparsely furnished but bright and clean and instead of railway lines it looked out on small but neatly kept gardens. A far cry from the last few months. Maureen and Peter Onslow were a bright young couple with a baby, prepared to accept Anne but hoping she wouldn't encroach too much on their own lives. Had they but known Anne they would have understood that all she wanted was to keep her distance. The past had taught her more than she knew for she was a model lodger, a gift from heaven.

To the dentist she surpassed herself, not having realised before that she could be completely efficient if she put her mind to it and she had no intention of losing this job. Once or twice she debated writing home. No, she would wait until she was doing even better. Apart from the occasional outings with Ted and the pictures with Rosie her social life was nil. Christmas came. Ted had gone to his parents who were living down on the south coast. The Onslows insisted on her spending the day with them. All went well until the evening and then her hate flared up with added violence, all because of a silly, elderly aunt who was all sweetness and light and insisted on being kind to that rather nice coloured girl. Anne was carrying a tray of glasses to the kitchen when she heard the quavering voice above the chink of crockery.

'She really is quite pleasant and I do feel we should be understanding, but I don't think it is really wise now Donald has finished at University and will be coming to London. I thought he would be living with Maureen and Peter.'

'You're right.' This voice was younger and more dominant and Anne knew it was that of a cousin, a very strong-minded woman. 'I believe we should always be kind but it is wrong to mix too freely. Especially young people. You never know what may happen and I don't believe in mixed marriages under any circumstances. It's the children. They say they always have the worst side of both parents. And they may seem perfectly nice and ordinary on the surface but you never know when they will revert.'

It was the first Anne had heard of Donald and she hadn't the faintest idea who he was nor wanted to know. She pushed open the door with her foot and walked into the room. Two pairs of startled eyes looked at her coldly angry face. Suddenly Anne smiled, the bitter smile that could look almost dangerous.

'It's terrible, isn't it? Just savages under the skin and we even eat our young!' She put the tray down on the table and turned towards the door.

'My dear,' the quavering voice rose a tone higher and shook a little more. 'I am really sorry. It was stupid of us and most unkind.'

Anne turned and faced them again. 'Don't bother to apologise. You spoke what you think is the truth and the ignorance of the English no longer amazes me. The only thing left is for us to pity your stupidity.'

She went straight up to her room. Half an hour later there was a knock on her door.

'Who is it?' she asked.

'Maureen. May I come in?'

'If you wish.'

Maureen's young face was troubled and there was no doubt that she had been crying.

'My aunt has told me what happened and I've come to apologise, although I gather they tried to do that themselves. Anne, do believe me when I tell you that I wouldn't have had this happen for anything. They didn't mean to be unkind, but they are old and set in their ways. They don't understand this modern world. You must know Peter and I feel quite differently or we would never have had you here.'

'Forget it.' There was no relenting in Anne's voice. 'I'm getting used to ignorance since I came to England. I'll get out as soon as possible.'

'Please, Anne, couldn't we start again?'

Anne was in no mood to accept any olive branch, however well meaningly it was offered.

'No thank you.'

Ted had only heard of the Onslows through a friend, so hadn't the faintest idea of what had happened and when he came back after Christmas Anne said nothing. She looked through the local paper for a room to let, looked on boards outside of shops, phoned, called and wrote to no avail. It was three weeks of steady plodding before she found a room to let at 22 Lenning Road. The room was clean and pleasant with a gas ring and a basin with hot and cold water and a bathroom on the same floor. Here she could be completely independent. She could even ask Rosie round for the evening.

It was the end of the first week and she had had a tiring day. She had become used to the work, she even liked it. People were pleasant and reasonably helpful, but today there had been several cancellations, a number of emergencies, including a child that screamed loudly the whole time it waited, the nurse had been irritable and Mr. Blake, the dentist, in a sheer bad temper. As she went into the hall a door at the back opened and a big man with a crop of fair hair stood staring at her. He was in his shirt sleeves and his hands thrust into the top of his trousers. He smiled, showing a set of white, even teeth.

'Hullo, so you're the new lodger! Well I'm blessed.' His voice was slightly slurred. 'The missus never said what a pretty little thing you were. How about coming in for a cup of tea?'

So that was Mrs. Morris's husband! Anne gave him a frigid look.

'No, thank you.' She walked towards the stairs, but he was there quickly, moving with the speed of a boxer. As she put her hand on the rail his large one covered it and when she glanced down she saw the stiff, fair hairs standing up aggressively. Her stomach revolted.

'Come on, dearie, you can't be as standoffish as that!' Suddenly he was behind her and his arms went round her and his big hands found her breasts. She kicked backwards in anger and something close to panic. Her stiletto heel caught his shin and he gave a gasp of pain but he didn't let go. She tried to reach down and bite his arm but she couldn't manage it. Then she found her voice.

'You filthy brute, let me go or I'll scream the house down.'

'I shouldn't do that. Who's going to believe a little coloured bint when I say you egged me on?'

'I would, Mr. Morris, and I think your wife would believe me even if I, too, have a coloured skin.'

The hands dropped away from her. The coloured man, who was now halfway down the stairs, was even bigger than Mr. Morris and there was a quietly determined expression on his face. Mr. Morris muttered something about having had a couple of drinks and was sorry if there had been a bit of a misunderstanding. He went towards the back of the house with the air of a dog that has been scolded. Anne hung on to the banister, suddenly aware that her legs were shaking. The dark face smiled gently.

'I'm sorry that happened. He probably had had a couple of drinks and got a bit amorous. Actually he's scared sick of his wife. Come along and I'll give you a cup of coffee.'

4

Anne walked up the stairs by Jeff's side. Her legs were still shaking. But it was gratifying to have another reason to hate the English. Jeff's room was immediately above hers. Before they went up the last flight he paused.

'You go on up. My door is open and the coffee on. I went down to get my milk and forgot it when I saw our Mr. Morris in the role of the great lover. Silly idiot. He'll have a fit now in case I should be misguided enough to tell his wife. I won't be a minute.'

She was sitting in the one armchair when he came in.

He saw the long, slim legs, the hands gripping the arms of the chair in obvious tension and the lovely face with the hard line of the lips. He thought she was still frightened.

'There's no need to be scared. He wouldn't have done anything more than get a bit fresh. Anyhow, his wife is seldom out for long.'

'Scared! Who said I was scared? I'm just flaming mad, that's all. Damn all white men! Think that if you've got a brown skin they can do as they like.'

'That's carrying it a bit far. They're not all the same, any more than we are. Have a cup of coffee and you'll feel better.'

In an effort to change the conversation he told her he had just bought the percolator and was trying it for the first time. Suddenly he realised he was very out of practice with small talk particularly with a pretty girl. He looked at her again. Her hands still gripped the chair and her mouth was closed tightly. He didn't like her! That was for sure! There was a hardness that repelled. Suddenly he saw Lucy sitting there in her place, warm and gentle with kind eyes, a full mouth and big, soft breasts. It was the first time he had seen her so clearly in his mind for months and months. Pain ran through him, slicing deeply, but today it seemed he was feeling pain with an intensity he had almost forgotten existed. He wanted Lucy, he wanted the children, wanted his parents with a longing that was a constriction of the throat and griping in the stomach. An agony of mind, heart and body. He turned back to the milk. Give this girl her coffee and let her get out. He mustn't drift any longer, he must make that effort, stop making excuses about time. If he had had enough guts he would have written a book by now.

'I'm Jeff Anderson from Malagai. I've been here over a year now.'

'I'm Anne Hunter and I've been here two years and more.'

She drank her coffee and still sat there, eyeing him thoughtfully until he felt she was weighing him up to his detriment and he grew hot under the collar.

Actually she was intrigued, wondering if he had a wife or a girl and if not why not? He was far above average in height and breadth but there was something not altogether masculine in his make-up. Now what? Her shrewd, calculating eyes took in every detail. Exceptionally good-looking, his dark skin smooth as satin apart from a scar on his cheek and another over his left brow, eyes large and clear, mouth gently curved, almost too gently for a man. Even when closed it was soft and full, instead of hard and straight. A man with a great deal of tenderness and imagination, but she doubted if he had much drive.

Now she knew why he was not wholly masculine. He might have an exceptionally good brain but he lacked force —that hard streak needed to be a complete success. What he needed was some of her own toughness! Her mouth curved up in an unexpected smile. If she knew where she was going she would damn well get there! Jeff saw the smile and felt a little more friendly towards her.

'No people here?' he asked in order to break that steady, scrutinising gaze.

'A cousin in Wales, that's all.'

'At least you have somewhere to go for your holidays.'

She laughed. 'No, thank you. I stayed with them when I first came over and they bored me to tears. Too full of good works for me.' Then she began to talk. Nothing about her home at all. Just the jobs she had had, the places she had lived in, the people she had met since she came to England, and through it all he could feel the hard core of hate. It was as if flood-gates had opened, as indeed they had and he

68

was astonished. She was such a child to hate so avidly.

'I know who you are now.' It came out unexpectedly, as did most things with Anne. 'I remember all the fuss last year about the way you were attacked and the articles you wrote for the *Meteor*. When I read them I felt slightly sick. All the loving kindness you had received from the old folk was so phony. Did the paper make you write such slush? You know, gentle coloured man being grateful for the crumbs dropped from the white man's table. Bearing no malice for the rough treatment. All sweet and sickly.'

He stared at her. 'Did you really think that? As a matter of fact it was just the opposite. The editor complained that it was too mild and added a little to make it sting. But it was just one of those unfortunate incidents and not indicative of general feeling. Some English hate us, some get on well with us and some are completely indifferent.'

'Good Lord, I believe you mean it!'

'Of course I do.'

'What are you doing now? I haven't seen your name to an article since. Don't tell me you are on the staff and the editor's blue-eyed boy.' The amusement in her voice stung.

'I'm afraid not, but it's largely my own fault. I haven't written much since.'

'According to the paper you are a writer of distinction. And you've given it all up. Don't tell me you are doing good works.' The sarcasm bit deep.

'No, it gave me up.'

'As soon as you were no longer news. Aren't the English marvellous? They use us when it suits them. London Transport would probably come to a halt if we all went back and who would sweep the streets, but don't try and get above your station whatever you do!'

'But I thought you were a dentist's receptionist and getting good money.'

'Because there is a shortage of receptionists, that's all. I'll bet you had the devil of a time looking for work.'

It was so annoyingly true and yet he couldn't work up a resentment about it as this girl could work up a hate that was like white-hot steel. Probably he hadn't enough character to do anything. He was still conscious that he disliked her, but she was interesting. A girl with force and drive if it were channelled in the right direction. She could make something of her life. The urge to get her interested in something outside of herself grew strong. He wondered what her home background was like. A broken home, an unmarried mother? It was nearly midnight when she went to her room and by then they had arranged to go out together on Sunday morning.

Jeff found himself looking forward to it with no sense of warning whatsoever and when it came they walked in the park. It was cold but dry and they talked and argued, argued and talked. And it was of nothing that happened before they came to England. Anne did not even tell him from which island she came and he didn't ask. It was as if neither of them had had any lives whatsoever until then and neither of them could have said why this happened. But they both began to come alive. To feel a tingle in the nerve endings which hadn't been there for a long time—if ever. A glow which was no bigger than the flame of a match, but it lit the morning. Perhaps it was because they both missed their own kind and had found nothing to replace them and there was no more to it than that. If Jeff had thought about it he would have said that he had far more in common with Lizzie and Alf, Doris and Reg, than he had with this girl with her bitterness and ill-concealed hate. Up to a point it was true. Anne was well aware that she understood Ted, with his hard common sense, more than she did Jeff, but being with him was a warmth that Ted could not give. It was the feeling of blue seas, warm sunshine, white sands, glittering moonlight and stars so bright and close you could pluck them out of the skies and fasten them in your hair. It was unspoken knowledge, but it was there just the same.

In the afternoon Jeff was on duty and he went to work with a smile. Anne went to meet Ted. He now knew about her leaving the Onslows and was furious and said so. At the same time he saw there was something different about her. Something warmer and more friendly, but she never mentioned Jeff. He thought perhaps she was wiser after all. Living on her own might be better for her.

He took her to dinner in a quiet little restaurant in Soho. She was damnably pretty! He wondered what his parents would think if they knew he was running around with a coloured girl. They were gentle and kind but very conservative. He wished to God she had a profession. They might take more kindly to her if she was a doctor or a nurse. The thought staggered him. Anyone would think he was serious! Well, he wasn't. She was interesting, she was pretty and he liked her tough streak. It showed character. She was a bit of an idiot in some ways, but she was young and she would learn and she was sticking her job.

'Have you seen anything of Rosie?'

'I went to the pictures with her last week. She loves her work and the children. All that talk of getting on in the world isn't likely to come to anything now. She and Jim are going steady.'

'To Rosie she has gone up in the world.' He was suddenly serious. 'She is already learning to speak what at one time she would have called "proper", she's out of the rut and Jim

71

is doing well. She'll end up a good wife in a middle-class home and enjoy every minute of it.'

'I suppose so, but it sounds deadly dull to me.'

'And what do you propose to do with your life, Anne, now you've stopped behaving like a fool and drifting from one rotten job to another? Save the money and go home at some time?'

'Perish the thought!' And yet the sunshine! What was she going to do? For long enough she had just got by, now she was earning a reasonable wage in a fairly interesting job. Keeping a roof over her head and food in her stomach had been her main object, but now there was the future. What chance had she got of doing anything else?

'Penny for them?'

She looked across the table. 'For what?'

'Your thoughts, of course.'

'I don't know what I am going to do. Unless I do something I suppose I shall go on taking down appointments for ever.'

'Better start thinking about it.' He grinned. 'I shall never forget the first time I met you. Scratching and spitting like a kitten that has been teased. Even now I am not sure if you had been teased or if you just happen to have a nasty disposition.'

'A nasty disposition.'

'But honest!'

'When it suits me.'

'I'm not so sure about that. I have a feeling you could be too honest for your own good.'

He drove her to her door and said he would let her know as soon as he was back in London. Anne went to her room and lit the gas fire. A little later she heard Jeff moving around on the floor above her. When she first met Ted she had deliberately used him to get a better job, thinking of him as a meal ticket and a stepping stone. She knew now that Ted had seen through her more clearly than she had thought and had only been used as much as he wanted to be. He'd had a good education, seen something of the world, knew what he was doing and there was money in the family. She could do worse than marry him—if he wanted to marry her, and she doubted it. If she made up her mind to marry him she would have to play her cards well and it would be a way of settling the future. She might even write home and tell her father, but she doubted if he would approve.

She sat and thought about it objectively, as if she was considering a new frock. She wasn't in love with Ted, but they understood each other. Neither of them was likely to let their feelings run away with them. If they married she would do her best to be a good wife in every way and she would like to have children. It hit her suddenly. Michael and Colin. She didn't damn well want more out of life than a home and children. Never before had she realised what a fool she had been. Had she stayed home and put up with Lydia or stuck a job she would, in time, have met someone she liked and married. Her own home and children. Did the man matter all that much? She didn't really think so. Her own mother had adored her children but she never remembered her taking much interest in her father or his work.

Lydia, Lydia, the fool, doted on him. How it had annoyed her to see her face light up when she heard his footstep and to see her father adoring his new wife had enraged her. No, she wanted a home and children, wanted to enjoy them as her mother had done. A man who was congenial and could provide the things she wanted, that was all. She got up and made some tea. What in the world had set off this train of thought? Just that she had the future to consider. It was as simple as that. She knew, too, that if she wanted a thing she would get it, by hook or by crook. She wasn't Jeff. She wouldn't drift through life as she was sure he would do.

Upstairs Jeff was hanging up his clothes carefully. He, too, was wondering about the future. He saw no chance of promotion and the thought of spending years as a booking-office clerk became less and less attractive. He could gradually save the money and go home but what would he tell Lucy? And what job could he get at home? The idea was impossible. He must find another job. It wasn't so much the money as the feeling of having some sort of future, a future in which promotion would be a possibility.

Having folded his trousers carefully he now rolled them in a ball and pitched them across the room—a spasm of temper which he had not shown for years. How Lucy would smile. Why, why, after all this time, did his mind continually turn to Lucy? As if he didn't know! Take a walk, have a bath, do anything to get the thought out of his mind, the insistent, driving force of sex which seldom really troubled him.

He wondered what the girl, Anne, was doing this evening. This evening! It was midnight! He wanted to talk to her, to talk to anyone, do anything rather than be haunted by his own longing.

Picking up his trousers he put them on and then got into his jacket and overcoat and, walking down the side of the stairs so they wouldn't creak, let himself out of the house. He put his key in the lock in order to shut the door quietly. In spite of it, Anne, lying wakeful, heard him go down.

He walked blindly and at last found himself crossing Vauxhall Bridge in the early hours of the morning. A car full of youngsters slowed down and almost stopped.

For a moment he thought they were going to offer him a lift. A window slid down and two heads were thrust out. Raucous voices shouted, 'Go home, nigger!' and then the car moved on swiftly. He stopped in his aimless wandering. A stranger in a strange land, unwanted. He stood uncertain. Utter despair swamped him. Where was he going, what was he doing with his life? He was farther away from his goal than he had been twelve months ago. He wondered if he had a goal. Lucy, the children, his parents! They were in totally different worlds. Would they ever meet again? He leant his arms on the parapet and stared down at the black water. A hand touched his shoulder.

'Hardly the time to be hanging around, man. Where are you off to?'

The policeman was smallish, his voice quiet, but there was the usual air of authority. For a moment Jeff had the insane longing to shake the hand from his shoulder and run. Mentally he heard the whistles and could see a crowd of policemen closing in.

'It's all right, officer, I'm just walking.' The gentle voice, the quiet manner, had its effect.

'Not a sensible time to be walking. I saw the car slow down. Obviously they were not asking if you wanted a lift.'

'Hardly.'

'Where do you live?'

He gave his name and address.

'Is there anything wrong? Bad news or anything?'

'No, I just couldn't sleep.'

'You're a long way from home. My beat goes part of the way and perhaps you can pick up a taxi. Come along, I'll walk with you.'

Obediently he walked by the policeman's side. He was right. It was a long way from home. A long, long way. Not to Lenning Road but to Lucy and the children. That was where home was.

A taxi came by and the policeman hailed it.

'Take this gentleman to Lenning Road.' He leant close to Jeff and whispered, 'You all right for money? He'll want a bloody big tip at this time of night.'

Jeff grinned, suddenly seeing the funny side. What a way to save money, taking a taxi home in the small hours, but he felt better, more at peace with himself.

'He'll get it and thank you. I feel better for your company.'

He stretched out on his bed even more exhausted than on the night he arrived. The sense of peace promptly vanished. He was a hopeless failure and he knew it was mainly his own fault. Would he ever get out of the rut? He would need a lot more self-discipline than he had used up till now. He was too tired and too despondent to be troubled by any yearning for Lucy's arms and soft, warm breasts. Reggie. He missed Reggie. He was a clot. He would write tomorrow and tell him he would take a job in his factory if he could get him one. More money and less expenses. He would begin to save again and have time to write. Reggie and Doris would see to that! In the meantime he would write an article on how England impressed him after eighteen months. He fell asleep and scarcely stirred until it was time to go to work.

He ran into Anne on his way home. She was laden with shopping and he took the basket from her hands. Heavens, how thin she was! He hadn't noticed it before. Women should have curves in the right places. Probably didn't eat enough or had this craze for slimming. Idiotic. Women were meant to be plump.

'Come and have something to eat with me,' she said, 'unless you are going somewhere.'

He went submissively. If he liked the girl there would be some sense—or would there? Tonight she was more relaxed, a smile came more easily, but in between her mouth shut in that hard line which he found so unattractive. They talked and he told her about some water-colours he had seen in the Victoria and Albert.

'They made me wish I was an artist.'

'And you could put your pictures in an art gallery and sell them for enormous sums, buy a house at Hampstead and show the world what the poor black man can do.'

'You never really let up, do you? Why?'

'I don't know. Probably because there is nothing I really want to do and I wonder how I will end up.'

'Don't we all?'

'You can write if you want to. I think you're afraid to try again in case you don't succeed.'

She was so right. Those rejection slips had taken the heart out of him and he had lost hope. But other people must have had them and had gone on and on until they succeeded.

'I'm right, aren't I?'

He nodded.

'Not much guts, have you? If I had real talent in anything I'd set the world on fire. I haven't any talent, only a very spiteful nature. Perhaps that's why.' She began to laugh and to his surprise it was rich and musical. 'Inside me is a frustrated artist or poet or something and it can't get out so I'm chewed up with hate of anyone and everyone.'

She sat on the divan and curled her long, thin legs under her, her dark head leaning against the wall, the smoke of her cigarette drifting around her, giving a dreamlike quality to her stillness.

For the first time a warning bell rang somewhere in Jeff's

head. He felt danger, wanted to run but could not. The contempt in her words, 'Not much guts, have you?' pricked the bubble of what was left of his self-esteem and he wanted to show her he was more than a drifting, gutless West Indian.

She stubbed out her cigarette and stretched herself, her lips curling with sardonic amusement as she looked at him.

The hard, bitter core was utterly unwomanly and yet the white-hot hate drew him like a moth to a flame. It was as if he bathed in the warmth of her fire in an effort to absorb some of her force. Subconsciouly he felt that if he could do that his life would take on purpose.

Suddenly she gave a totally different smile, free from sarcasm and bitterness.

'The only things I don't hate are children and Rosie.'

'Who is Rosie?'

She told him about Rosie and he saw a half-ashamed tenderness. So she had her vulnerable spots, after all. And still they never mentioned their lives before they came to England.

The letter to Reggie was never written and the article not even started. Instead Jeff found himself spending more and more time with Anne. They went to a five-shilling dance where they discovered that the latest dances were completely outside of their knowledge and were reduced to helpless laughter. A young West Indian couple came up to them and tried to be friendly, but after a while they gave up and went away. They went to the pictures, had meals in small cafés. If Jeff had found it difficult to save before it was even more difficult now. The places they went to didn't amount to much, yet the money slipped through his fingers and the day came when he drew a little on the money he had received from the first articles.

He cashed the cheque with a pain in his heart, feeling this was the beginning of the end. Lucy and the children didn't seem to belong any more and he was a man on his own. A man spending far too much time with a girl. His letters home were becoming more and more brief and yet he wanted Lucy more than he had ever done. A lifeline slipping out of his grasp. The miserable thing was that his feelings for Anne were so mixed. He wanted to be with her and yet there was so much about her he didn't even like. Her pungent, cutting remarks flicked him on the raw. Sometimes he told himself that he must call a halt to the friendship but as usual he let life take care of itself.

Ted came back to London for a week. He was rushed off his feet, but he saw Anne at every opportunity. One evening they were at his favourite restaurant, a little Hungarian place in Soho. Dimly lit, intimate and excellent food. Anne was smiling at him. She had altered subtly, but for the life of him he could not say how and she did not even know there was a difference yet. She made excuses to Jeff that she had a friend staying in London and would be booked up, not mentioning his sex or his nationality. Jeff was fine to go out with but there was no future in it. She suspected there was a wife back home, but nothing was said and she was determined to have security and the happiness of a home. Jeff was a pleasant companion and no more. Ted was the future. So she calculated and Ted, just as careful, calculated, too.

Marriage had not been a serious thought with any other girl, but Anne attracted him in a way no other had done. He wasn't sure if he was in love with her, but he wanted her, he knew that, but she wasn't the girl for an affair, he knew that, too. Would it be better to stop seeing her? He was no prude, but even if she was the sort to have an affair he had an overwhelming feeling it would be wrong. She was a stranger in a strange place without the protection of home and relatives. Unexpectedly a deep tenderness rose in him. You'd have to be a dreadful swine not to think of that. When he first met her he had been amused at her spitefulness but now pity rose. Something must have hurt her badly in the past. He no longer felt it was her natural disposition. Besides, in these evenings he had often caught a tender smile in her eyes and on her lips.

'Job going well, Anne?'

'A-ha!'

'It's made a lot of difference to you, hasn't it?'

'There are no dirty old men or smart young toughs to run their fingers up my arm and think I should be grateful for their attentions.' A touch of the old hate but, in a way, he liked it. She was no milk-and-water miss, she had spice. He wondered about her home. Did she write or had she cut herself off completely? He wanted to know more about her background.

During that week he managed to draw her out more and neither realised the other was being calculating. Her father was a lawyer. He'd married again after her mother died. She told him about her home, she even went so far as to tell him about Lydia and admitted that she was part of the reason why she had come to England but was too shrewd to tell him how she hated her. Too shrewd to say anything against her. It was a game of chess in which each covered their moves carefully.

He drove her to Lenning Road and as he helped her out of the car he bent and kissed her lightly for the first time. 'I'll drop you a line and see you soon,' he murmured, then watched her run up the steps and let herself into the front door.

Jeff was coming home from late shift and saw the whole incident. His long legs carried him at a terrific rate and by the time Anne was opening her own door he was by her side and she was in his arms. It was utterly uncalculated, he couldn't stop himself. His own need for love and comfort, her attraction which was mixed with a queer dislike and screaming, aching, longing for Lucy and a wild, unreasoning jealousy. There was no thought, just primitive instinct brought to the surface because he had seen another man kiss her.

'I thought you hated all white men,' he muttered. 'Not enough to make you stop one kissing you! So that's the friend you've been seeing all the week. You're a liar.'

'He's never kissed me before, really, Jeff.' She was murmuring the words against his mouth, forgetting how she had been angling for a secure future with Ted. She was thinking of nothing but Jeff and his closeness, the strength of his arms and the closeness of his mouth.

Her door was partly open and Jeff pushed it with his foot, still holding Anne they went inside and he pushed it shut and again his lips found hers, eager in their seeking. She stayed in his arms and slowly her lips responded and her calculating mind gave way to his urgent loving. Wave after wave of longing surged through her thin body. This was something outside of her understanding. Her arms went round his neck and she clung, passionately. Dear Lord, she loved him, loved him to the exclusion of her brain, to the exclusion of everything. Nothing mattered, nothing but this love and need. He carried her to the divan still kissing her, one minute with great tenderness, the next with deep passion. She murmured, 'Oh, Jeff, Jeff I love you, I love you,' but he didn't answer.

The love-making grew until it caught them in wild ecstasy. Nothing, nothing mattered in the whole world but their two selves.

Hours later she lay sleeping peacefully, her head on his

shoulder, and Jeff lay wakeful. Now, his sex instincts satisfied, his conscience was awake and he hated himself with a bitterness that gnawed at his vitals. What on earth had possessed him? Animal instinct! It was the most devastating feeling. He wanted to go and bathe as if that could wash away some of the shame he felt, but he couldn't waken her. She looked like a child with her small face and thin body. Lucy, Lucy! Thank heaven there was none of Lucy in this girl to remind him of those soft, warm breasts and gentle love and yet he could not stop thinking of her. This girl was a creature of passion and fire, not deep tenderness. He had let Lucy down in every way now. By fear, indolence over his work, by lack of trying and now by uncontrolled sex. And he had vowed he would never be unfaithful to Lucy by even a moment's thought!

He looked down at the sleeping face. Her black, curling hair lay like a dark cloud on the white pillow, the brown lids were closed smoothly over the full eyes, the long, black lashes lay on the silky cheeks like tiny, feather fans, the mouth was no longer closed in a thin line but full and rich. His feelings were a mixture of sad pity and complete helplessness. What was he going to do? How in the name of heaven was he going to cope?

Perhaps, when she wakened, the answer would be in her eyes. Perhaps she, too, had been merely caught up in the same passion which was an outcome of loneliness and near despair. Despair because they were both captives in a land which offered them little opportunity or hope. Despair because those they loved were so far away and out of their reach. Perhaps she would waken full of regrets for what had happened. He lay quite still, determined to let her sleep until she wakened naturally. It was the least he could do.

5

Anne opened her eyes slowly. Rain was pattering on the window. She moved her head gently, nestling a little closer to Jeff's huge shoulder. There was no wondering what happened. She remembered every detail acutely. Now she knew why her father had married Lydia and hate dropped away. Lydia had given him what her mother never had to give. Something she had not thought possible. She was her father's child, after all. She felt she should write and tell him that she understood now and that she was coping with life very well. Nothing mattered but this all encompassing love. She moved her head and looked up at Jeff to see if he was still asleep. The expression in his eyes puzzled her and then she thought she understood. Poor darling, he was ashamed. Instinctively she knew there was a puritanical streak somewhere in his make-up and the silly man felt terrible. Her smile was pure amusement. For a moment he felt a sense of sheer relief. She, too, had been caught up in an unexpected passion. There was no more to it than that. It must never happen again. He would move away and the affair would end. But her words brought havoc.

'Jeff, darling, I'm so happy. I love you, love you, love you and I didn't think I could love anyone like it. It's a heavenly day and the world is my oyster. Oh, look at the time! I must hurry. I can't afford to lose my job.'

She was out of bed like a whirlwind, gathering her clothes together.

'Dearest, are you working today?'

He shook his head.

'Then be an angel and make coffee. I must have my

coffee. I don't come awake until then. I'll have a quick bath.' She drew the curtains and looked out at the rain-washed street. 'It's raining. Not to worry. I won't be more than ten minutes and then we can have our coffee quietly.'

'I'll make it in my room. Could you come up there?'

He didn't want her to, he wanted time to think, but there was nothing he could do about it and he had the day ahead for all the thinking. When she was out of the room he got into his clothes and went upstairs, praying no one would see him, but he needn't have worried. Nobody was around. Once in his attic room he put on the perco-lator and in a few moments the pungent smell filled the air. What was he going to say when she came up? It had all been a hideous mistake? He was bitterly ashamed? It had happened partly because of his need for Lucy. But he couldn't speak of Lucy to Anne. It would have seemed like sacrilege. The awful thing was that Lucy had gone so far from his mind for so long. He had found it even difficult to picture her, but now she was there, in front of him, as real and as near as she had been on that last night he had held her in his arms. It didn't make sense. It was almost as if she had deserted him instead of the other way round. She had left him until he was caught in a trap (albeit of his own making) and then she was there again. Sad-eyed, unhappy, accusing.

Anne ran up the stairs singing softly. Jeff was standing by the window, staring out at the rain. Nothing but grey roofs and cold, sad, English rain. He didn't hate it. It just filled him with sick longing for the sea and sun-kissed sands. Anne rushed across the room and flung herself against him, winding her arms around him, pressing her-self against his big body and laughing.

'Jeff, Jeff, I'm so happy. I never thought it was possible, although I should have known all these weeks. There's

84

been another feeling ever since I've known you, but I didn't know I could feel like this. It's as if there is another me inside who has become suddenly free. A me who was a prisoner without even knowing I was there. I wish I hadn't got to go to work because it's our honeymoon.'

She was such an astonishing person. Immaturity and maturity together. She didn't say, 'Do you love me?' as most women would. She took it for granted. She loved, therefore the love must be returned.

The milk boiled over, which gave him respite. She drank her coffee scalding hot and neither of them mentioned food.

'I've got to run. Take care of yourself, darling. I'll be back as quickly as I possibly can. No later than six. It may be earlier. Then we can talk and talk.'

She was gone and he sank in the armchair with the coffee by his side. He didn't know what to do. Would it be better to be out when she came home? To stay out, do anything to avoid her? That was the coward's way. No, he would have to be waiting, have to talk, have to tell her he had been a heel. He didn't love her, had no love to give. In the meantime get out, do something, stop thinking. Why hadn't he contacted Reg, done anything rather than let this happen, and yet it had been too sudden to warn him that it could. But had it? These last weeks he should have thought instead of drifting. But wasn't that what he had done all his life? He had stayed on the *Vanguard* when he should have been struggling to do more. His epitaph would be, 'Jeff Anderson, who drifted through life.'

He went to the Commonwealth Institute and wandered round and round, looking carefully at the exhibits and seeing nothing. By five o'clock he was back in Lenning Road, waiting. Physical courage was so easy, mental courage so hard. He prayed that she would come quickly, while he had worked himself into the state of being able to tell her what was in his mind.

By five-thirty she hadn't come and in the next half-hour any courage he had instilled into himself slowly evaporated. The nearby church was striking six when he heard her heels clicking on the stairs. He had left the door ajar because he dare not open it knowing she would fling herself into his arms. It made no difference. She dropped her parcels on the table and was across the room before he could do anything about it. What could he say? 'I'm a swine! I don't love you at all. You're not even a passable stand-in for Lucy. Half the time I don't even like you. Let's forget it and say goodbye.'

Lucy, Lucy! How often had her name been in his heart these last hours? It should have been there continually and he might have been safe.

Anne sensed nothing wrong and slowly his arms tightened round her. Not because he wanted her but because his own helplessness forced him to do what he told himself he shouldn't.

'I'm later than I intended because I stopped at the supermarket. You can hardly live on love, although I feel that I could.'

'You had better not try. You are too thin now.'

'Am I?' She was unperturbed, certain of herself.

Most women, he thought, would have been slightly troubled by the remark and promptly wanted to know if they really were too thin or too fat or whatever he happened to say. He remembered an occasion in which he had teased Lucy about the size of her bottom and she had gone on a diet until he assured her he liked her that way. Anne was the complete egoist and in a way it was touching.

'I've been thinking.' She was hurrying round the room,

laying the table, getting the meal ready, as if she had been doing it for him all her life. 'We should get a place together away from here.' She looked at him quizzically. 'I suppose you can't marry me?'

He shook his head miserably. She completely misunderstood.

'I thought that was what was wrong or you would have asked me to marry you before last night. Don't worry, we'll get by. I wonder if we could get a flat among our own people. Here we stand out like a sore thumb. If we stay on somebody is bound to find out and we will probably be told to go anyhow. I imagine Mrs. Morris is a bit of a prude. And if we get a flat together it will be so much more economical.'

She had it all worked out. The idea of marrying Ted for security had gone completely. What a daft idea that had been! No, she would work out the future. Now there was something to work for. She and Jeff. If Jeff had been another type, had made passes at her, dropped hints, she would never have been so sure, but it had hit him as it had hit her, like a clap of thunder, devastating. She was as certain of that as she was that it had been teeming with rain all day. He couldn't marry her, so what! It would work out. She talked on, not even noticing his silence. She ate with real enjoyment, Jeff ate because the food was there in front of him and he had eaten nothing all day, but it was as dust and ashes in his mouth. He murmured yes and no like a robot, feeling as if he were putty in Anne's hands, which were suddenly and frighteningly capable.

'You know, Jeff, once we can find somewhere to live together I'm going to start studying. Goodness knows what. I've never shown any talent for anything. Do you think it would better to work for my G.C.E. or take shorthand and typewriting? Of course, that would be useful when you start writing again. I could help you.'

She was arranging their lives as calmly and efficiently as if they were married. The girl who could hate with such force and bitterness could use that force for other things and he should have known that. Just as she took it for granted that from now on they would arrange their lives together, so she took it for granted they should, from now on, sleep together.

Suddenly, like a boy, he panicked, stuttering and stammering, trying to find the words. This was a risk he should never had let her take last night and they dare not risk it again. They did not want . . . Words failed. She took him up with all the calm of a woman who had been married for years.

'Don't be silly, Jeff, I'm not a fool. I don't want to have a baby like that. It would be stupid. That's another reason why I was late. I'm not exactly a fool and it's quite safe now.' Suddenly she was shy. 'Don't think I've ever given myself to anyone else. I haven't. I've never wanted to.'

He felt worse than ever. Almost as if he had raped her with brute force. But supposing, just supposing! Anything could have happened last night! His mind was tortured. He was a fly caught in a spider's web, but when he looked at her he knew that was not true. He was the culprit, not Anne. He bowed under his own helplessness and guilt. He couldn't say the words he intended, he couldn't. Perhaps it would work itself out. He gave way under the inevitable.

'We'll look for a flat.'

He went to work the next morning with the guilt of the whole world on his shoulders. No longer did he think of how he could explain to Anne. Thank heavens that finding a flat was far easier said than done. He hung on to that thought with a vague hope that while they were still in Lenning Road there might be a chance that Anne would think better of it. It was like Canute on the seashore.

But it was as if all the forces there were lined up against him. He was drinking coffee when Althea came and sat next to him. Althea from whom he had run like a rabbit. If only he had taken her up on her almost blatant offer. There would have been no ties there. She would have welcomed him to share her life on a temporary basis, being almost unperturbed when he left it again. She was no whore, just a woman who liked a man around the house for company and comfort. Cheeky, gay, affectionate, with no deep or abiding feelings. The future did not worry Althea. She'd got a job, a schoolgirl daughter and a home. The only thing missing was a man.

'Hullo, Jeff, haven't seen you in a long whiles.' Her grin was infectious. 'Do you know you did me the best turn any man ever did.'

He raised his eyebrows questioningly. She giggled.

'Well, I as good as made you an offer but you didn't take it up. At the time I was disappointed. I thought you were nice and would be good fun to live with and I didn't expect more. Well, I've met a man who wants to marry me. He's a bus-driver. A widower without any children and a little house in Tottenham. He doesn't mind that I've got a daughter and have been around. I can cook and clean and he doesn't want me to go out to work anymore. He's really nice. We're getting married next week. I suppose you wouldn't like to take my flat on? You can have it just as it stands. My friend says I can let it if it's to someone nice but he won't have it filled with a crowd.'

Althea and her 'nice'. It was her favourite word. He said he would be glad to without using his head at all. He didn't tell her there was a woman now.

89

That night he said nothing to Anne about it, it would have been too final. Besides, she might alter her mind about her feelings and if so the flat would be somewhere for him to go, somewhere to get away. He knew perfectly well he was kidding himself. They went to the pictures. He would have gone anywhere with her in order to stop her talking, stop her cheerful planning. When they came home she slept in his narrow bed as if it was the most natural thing in the world.

He was on early shift and had left for work before Anne was awake. Looking at the little hollows under her cheekbones and the fan of black lashes, Jeff felt deep compassion. She battered so hard at life. Would she end by battering herself to death against the rocks?

Anne wakened and stretched herself luxuriously. So Jeff had already gone. She wished he had wakened her so that she could have got up and made him some coffee. A day's work and she would be with him again. She met the day with glory. Her heart soared and the world was right. She had never noticed before how gentle Miss Stewart, the nurse, was. Her voice was soft, her eyes kind.

'You're looking prettier than ever this morning, Anne.' She was a small woman, her hair already greying. Time and again she had made an effort to be friendly but the girl had made no response but this morning her answering smile was quick.

'Do I? Thank you. Maybe I am in a better temper and it shows.'

Not just a better temper, thought Miss Stewart, she's happy and I don't think she has been before.

Anne's smile was warm and the patients smiled back. She was suddenly conscious that she no longer disliked the English with such dogmatic truculence. Life was easier and the time slipped by. It was four-thirty when the phone rang for what seemed like the thousandth time.

'Dr. Denham's surgery. Can I help you?'

'I jolly well hope so. Ted here.'

'I didn't expect you back in London yet.'

'I'm only in town for the evening and I have to leave early. What time will you be ready? I'll pick you up.'

If only he had given her some warning so that she could have told Jeff she might be late. She didn't want to see Ted, but she would have to if only to tell him she wouldn't be seeing him again. She felt no compunction about it, for they had been no more than good friends. The fact that she had intended to do her best to marry him was neither here nor there. She had better see him and make some excuse to get away quickly. Say she was meeting Rosie.

'I'll be ready at five-thirty.'

'Good girl. I'll be there on the dot.'

The car was a few yards down the road and Ted was standing by the door. He saw the difference in her immediately and thought it was on account of his unexpected visit. Her smile was warmer, her eyes alight, even her step had something gay about it. Pert, quick, like a young colt on a spring morning. His heart beat faster. He knew now he wanted to marry her and was glad he had told his parents of their friendship and asked them to meet her as soon as possible. Once she was in the car it was difficult not to take her in his arms. No, don't rush her, give her time.

'What's brought you up to London for such a short time?'

'Oh, this and that and you as well.' He threaded his way gently through the traffic. 'My mother would like you to come down for the weekend. This one if you can manage it. She would have sent you an invitation by post, but I've brought it myself.'

It was a pleasant, friendly note, saying how much she and her husband were looking forward to meeting her and giving time of trains both of arrival and departure. Anne knew Ted's mother was really afraid, hoping against hope there was no more than friendship between them. A week ago, this would have roused her ire, now it made her feel slightly ashamed. She had made up her mind to marry Ted for nothing more than security and the hope of having children. His mother would have sensed that and how could she be expected to love a prospective daughter-in-law under those circumstances? She liked Ted but she had never loved him in the smallest degree. She put the letter in her handbag.

'I'll answer it tomorrow. I'm sorry, Ted, but I won't be able to accept the invitation. I'm booked up.'

He glanced at her quickly, wondering if she was afraid of being criticised. Not like Anne. She was a fighter. On the other hand she possibly wanted to be a little more sure of herself and of him before she met his parents which was understandable. He turned into a side street and found a parking meter.

'If you can't manage this weekend, Anne, what about the next?'

'I'm sorry, Ted, I can't.'

'Is it because you think my parents won't approve? They know all about you. I've told them.' Once he had made up his mind he didn't believe in beating about the bush. 'Anne, we've been friends for some time now. I love you and want to marry you.' The words came out quickly because he knew now without the slightest doubt. He loved her, all the silly hate that had been like a torrent when he first met her was all part of her dynamic quality. Power to hate usually meant power to love in the same degree. Her love would be forceful and passionate. Not always easy to live with but he could cope.

Anne looked at him. The thick thatch of dark brown hair, the light grey eyes, the clear-cut features and strong jaw. Funny that she had never quite realised before how attractive he was. He was reliable, too, and would make a good husband. If he had said those words a week ago she would have said yes without a moment's hesitation— and what a rotten wife she would have been. Taking everything and giving little in return. You couldn't be a good wife without love, she knew that now, and she didn't love Ted. Ted had never seen her eyes so gentle and his heart bounded. Then she shattered his ego.

'I'm sorry, Ted, I can't marry you. I'm in love with someone else.'

'But Anne, you never mentioned anyone else before.'

'I know, but it all happened so quickly.'

'Then there isn't much I can say, is there?'

'No.'

'May I see you sometimes, keep in touch?'

There was no reason why they shouldn't meet sometimes. Ted had been kind, he had helped her when she needed it. Been honest and told her to pull herself together. Had it not been for him she might never have met Jeff. He told her he would ring her at the surgery when he was in London next. When he left her there was a feeling of loss. Would he ring, would she ever see him again? She had refused to let him take her back to Lenning Road because she wanted to get him out of her immediate thoughts.

Jeff was back early, his mind still muddled and worried. What was he going to do? He should be honest and tell Anne he didn't love her, it had been a mixture of loneliness and lust. It was a horrible thought and his puritanical mind boggled at the words, but he must, for both their sakes, break this affair up.

Six o'clock came and no Anne. Was she down in her room? He went down and knocked on the door but there was no answer. He turned on the radio and tried to concentrate on the news. There had been a stirring of racial troubles. Stories of Ku Klux Klan activities. Not here in England! He knew, only too well, that his people were not accepted by everyone, that many resented them, that some young toughs caused trouble, but then they were the type who were out for trouble of any sort. It was their way of calling attention to themselves. They wanted to be in the limelight. But surely the majority of English were gentler, had more common sense. Didn't they ever consider how they had encompassed the world? How they had gone to countries that were not their own, made money there, sometimes enslaved the people? There was no bitterness in his thoughts, just a wonder that there could be so little understanding. Why didn't those with knowledge and power explain how difficult it was to get work in the islands? He supposed the government was doing its best, but if only it would point out the why and the wherefore. There was still a labour shortage. Couldn't the English understand? His people did a thousand dirty jobs that Englishmen were beginning to reject. And what was he doing to help? Sitting down in his little corner and doing nothing to help himself let alone anyone else. He even avoided his own people.

Seven o'clock and still Anne didn't come. With the radio going he would not have heard those clicking heels on the stairs. Again he tapped on her door. Fear caught hold of him. Suppose she had been run over. So often in the past weeks he had caught her hand and held her back when she would have stepped into the road without thinking. She was so impetuous and careless. The thought of her being blotted out hurt unbearably and he knew that even if he wanted to escape her, even if there were moments in which he disliked her, there were others when she drew him to her in a bond which he could not understand. Was it a strange sort of love as well as passion? He went back to his room. Try to get her out of his thoughts. Think of all he should do with his life. Anne, Anne, with the large eyes and the thin, childish body. He thought of it crushed and lifeless under the wheels of some passing car, and shuddered, overwhelmed with fear and tenderness. Poor child, a creature of passion caught up in the maelstrom of life, thrown this way and that, incapable of getting into a quiet stream. He gave up all attempts to be rational and paced the floor. For the first time he thought of her as being his responsibility. He stopped thinking of himself and only thought of her. Should he inquire of the police? They would think he was out of his mind. He was no relation and he could hardly tell them the truth.

By half past seven he was frantic. It was eight-thirty when he heard her heels on the stairs and flung his door wide. Now anger came into it. How could she have let him worry so? Then he saw the quiet look in her eyes, as if she lost a great deal of her girlhood and become a woman. Relief flooded his body. She was safe!

'Anne.' He took her in his arms, everything else drained away. 'Where have you been? I was afraid you had met with an accident.'

'I'm sorry, Jeff, I couldn't help it. Something cropped up.' Darling, darling Jeff. She had not thought he loved her so much.

It was the beginning of a different relationship. He knew now that in some ways he loved her, not as he loved Lucy but with a clinging need and a tenderness for her youth, with a sad knowledge of his own frailty and a vague admiration for a strength and force he did not possess himself. But with that knowledge came also a sense of thankfulness. A sop to his self-esteem. He did love her, it wasn't just lust! For such small mercies can the human character be grateful!

6

Jeff and Anne moved into Althea's flat and Anne became a mixture of child and woman. Childishly thrilled to be sharing everything with him but unexpectedly capable in the way she took over the household duties. His clothes were washed and ironed with meticulous care, his buttons were all sewn on, and when he came back from work there was always food prepared even if she was unable to be there herself, for Jeff's hours were awkward.

And Jeff was torn all ways. He felt differently towards Anne now, he loved her, not as he did Lucy but with a compassionate tenderness and an admiration for her strength. He only wrote to Lucy when Anne was out of the flat and the letters were a penance. But that was not all. They were now living in a district where West Indians made up a large part of the community and he hated to go out for fear he should meet someone he knew when he was with Anne. How could he explain to her? He was quite aware that plenty of men were living with other women while their wives were back home, but that was no excuse for him. Suppose someone saw him and wrote to Lucy—or his parents! There were times when he was tempted to write and tell them himself and yet he couldn't bring himself to it. All he could do was to wait and hope a solution would come.

And now something else bothered him. Ever since they had moved to this district he had begun to think of the plight of some of his own people. It haunted him and yet he did not know what he could do.

If there had been no Anne he would now have gone out to meet them, tried to talk things over, to make some sort of effort towards better racial understanding but he had got himself into a position in which he could do nothing and his inner frustration ate him up. He didn't realise that had he not met Anne he might not have thought about it at all.

Anne felt his growing frustration but could not put her finger on what was troubling him. To her he was always gentle and loving although he always avoided telling her he loved her. It was as if that would have been the final disloyalty to Lucy for how could a man love two women at the same time?

Early summer was with them, clear and sunny, drawing the young couples into the parks, flooding the dull, grey streets with light, painting the skies blue. Anne gloried in it, seeing hope for the future in every splash of colour, her eyes were bright, her full mouth ready to smile at anything. Gone was the straight line of her lips and she no longer looked distrustingly on the world. Not that the world really mattered. She had her own little world, a world created out of her love and her imagination.

One evening she got home from work a little earlier than usual and found Jeff slumped in his chair with an open newspaper on his knees.

'What's wrong, darling, you look fed-up.'

He pointed to the article he had been reading. It was

on the now popular subject of race discrimination. Facts, hard, cold facts which added up to the stupidity of human nature, white and coloured alike.

'How, in heaven's name,' he asked, 'can we expect to live in peace when people continually stir each other up? It's like having thorns stuck into your body at intervals. When one stops hurting the other starts.'

'Well, there's nothing we can do about it. It will sort itself out.'

'I doubt it unless there is a real effort on both sides at greater understanding. There's a case here of a West Indian buying a house and then making life hell for an old couple who have lived there for years. Another case of a white landlord making life miserable for a coloured woman and her baby, to say nothing of charging an exorbitant rent. No thought for human suffering just how to make the most money in the least time. Nobody cares about human beings.'

'Well, we're West Indians and not exactly getting this place as a gift from the West Indian landlord and I bet he'd have charged more if you hadn't known his girl friend.' She grinned. 'I expect there are plenty of cases in which white landlords are swines to white tenants and white tenants breaking up the property of their landlords. I don't see why you should get so upset. It's just human nature to make money out of someone.'

She didn't see why he should get so upset. It was none of their business. Her detached attitude irritated Jeff out of all proportion, probably because he had never tried to do anything himself. Couldn't she see the dangers of the situation? For a few minutes they argued and then Anne suddenly said, 'Well, if you feel like that about it why don't you do something instead of just getting mad?'

'What do you think I can do?' Jeff was trying to contain his anger.

'You're a writer, aren't you? You should be able to do something. All you do is to brood about it.'

Just as if it was the easiest thing in the world. What was the sense of writing if nobody would print what you wrote? They were very near to an out-and-out quarrel and suddenly Anne threw herself into his arms with such passionate loving that he was swept out of his anger into the excitement and freedom from thought she could so quickly arouse. I can't fight her, she won't let me, he thought.

Lucy's letters were far less frequent and much more brief but they were still loving and told him all the news about his parents and the children but she said little about herself. He almost welcomed their infrequency for any letters from home were becoming a nightmare because Anne would look at him when they came. She said nothing but saw how he slipped them into his pocket to be read when he was alone and he knew it both hurt and angered her. He would read them carefully and then destroy them. But although Anne might be hurt and angry as the weeks went by he grew more and more dear and she had no intention of saying anything which might worry him if she could help it. Sometimes she would vaguely wish they could get married. It would make things so much simpler but she didn't care too much, just poured out her love regardless, convinced that everything would work out all right in the end. If it didn't it would not be for the want of trying on her part. Anne had gone a long way from the girl who had been prepared to marry Ted for the sake of a home and children. She no longer hated anyone, she just didn't care. She loved Jeff to the exclusion of all else. Just as she had been consumed by hate now she was consumed by love. She knew no half-measures.

Sometimes she would wake in the night and stretch her arms round his big body, her whole being suffused with love and tenderness. It seemed there had never been a time in her life when she hadn't loved him. There was nothing about him she didn't love, from his great, strong body, with its wide shoulders and narrow hips, to his sadly gentle eyes and the scar tissue on his cheek and forehead. But there were times when she was anxious, anxious for him, not herself, particularly since he seemed so worked up about this race-relation business. She thought the whole thing grossly exaggerated and very silly. The papers were making a fuss about nothing in order to increase their sales. Anne was the complete egoist. What did not affect her did not exist. But she must do something about Jeff. He must have an outlet for this fetish of his. She must do something to get him back to his writing. But how? If only she had someone to talk to but, like Jeff, she had shut herself in a walled garden, the only difference being that hers was full of flowers and his mainly thorns.

There was Rosie. Rosie, the only real friend she had ever made. They had seen less and less of each other of late. Rosie was full of her work. Once a week she went to evening classes and once a week she went out with Jim. Very occasionally she and Anne went to the pictures and Anne said nothing about Jeff, only that she now had a flat. She would have asked Rosie over when Jeff was working late, but it would have needed only half an eye to see she did not live alone. She didn't know why she hadn't told Rosie. She wasn't ashamed. Was it that deep down she felt that Jeff was not a wholly willing partner? That he had drifted into it because of a weakness in his own make-up?

Gradually Anne realised that she would have to provide the strength and the drive for both of them. She had talked blithely at first of taking classes in something or other but that would have to wait. Now it was Jeff that mattered. She racked her brains to think of some way to work a miracle.

Strangely enough it was a very simple incident that set her off. She had been to the pictures with Rosie. Rosie with her bright hair neatly cut, a simple tweed coat and flat-heeled shoes. She went out a lot with the children and it was better to dress plainly. The clothes made her flaring good looks even more noticeable. Rosie's speech had improved amazingly and Anne began to think Jim would have to look to his laurels or she would go beyond him.

They each went their separate ways and Anne was waiting on the almost deserted Tube platform for the theatres were not yet out as she and Rosie had gone to an early show. She stood there quietly, her mind on Jeff and his frustrations. A voice by her side said, 'Hi, all on your own?'

A coloured boy stood by her side, young, brash, with the bold eyes of a youngster entirely sure of himself and, what he considered, his charm. Anne gave him a cold stare.

'That,' she said, 'is my business,' and turned her back.

'Come along, baby, we're two of a kind. Why not get together?'

Her anger rose and the look she gave him was enough to wither the average male whatever colour, but this boy was made of sterner stuff.

'Come along, don't be high and mighty with me. We're in a strange country and we need each other.'

'I wouldn't need you on a desert island, you dirty bastard. Leave me alone.'

Her anger was a flame which warmed his eagerness and he grinned. Catching her arm he leaned forward.

'I like a girl with a temper. Something to tame.'

'Making a nuisance of himself, miss?' The man had come

up quietly. A pert little cockney with wrinkled face and pugnacious manner. 'You sheer off and leave the lady alone.'

The boy clenched his fists. 'Mind your own business and beat it, white man, or I'll break you in little bits.'

He could have done it, too, but several more passengers had come on to the platform and then a porter. A big, dark West Indian. He looked at the three standing close together and summed up the situation rapidly and suddenly he was angry.

'You again, is it?' He looked at the boy. 'Man, if I have more trouble with you pestering ladies down here I'll get the police.' A train drew into the station. The boy made as if to get on it. 'Oh, no, you don't. The lady gets on this train and you wait for the next. You all right?' He looked at Anne and she nodded.

Anne sat down in the carriage with the little cockney opposite. He smiled and she smiled back.

'Thank you for coming along.'

'That's all right. Get a bit above themselves, some kids. Parents don't seem to worry what they get up to these days.'

She didn't know the answer or pretend to, but if he wasn't careful that boy would end up in jail and then some silly West Indian would promptly blame it on to race relations when it was nothing of the sort. If there hadn't been anyone else around she had a nasty feeling that the little man opposite would have had the worst of it and she wouldn't have put it past that boy to swear he was protecting her. He was no better than the lads who had beaten Jeff.

Jeff was still out and she was sitting at the table writing when he came in. He looked at her in astonishment and then laughed.

'I began to think you couldn't write.'

'And I begin to think you can't.' She went on writing. 'The government are stopping some of the immigration and I don't wonder. Poor West Indians! Some of them want whips to their nasty backs.' She launched into a spirited and rather exaggerated account of the incident. Jeff stared at her. 'Now tell me the poor boy is deprived in some way. It couldn't possibly be that he is just a nasty little bastard, could it? Well, I'm going to write to the papers and say it is high time they sent a whole heap back and then some of us might be accepted more easily. I don't wonder some of the English hate our guts.'

'Anne, you can't do that.'

'Why can't I?'

'It would stir up trouble.'

'So what? Why should some of the worst come over here and give people the impression that we're all a lot of uncouth savages? Don't look at me. You're the writer. If you think it is the fault of conditions here why don't you write a book about it? Tell people about some of the coloured men's problems and you'd better add something about the white men's, too. I'm only just beginning to see that it isn't all one-sided. I've a nasty feeling that if no one else had come along that little old man that came to my rescue might have ended up under the train.' She didn't really think that, but she was intent on putting some fire into Jeff. He looked at her miserably.

'How can I write about problems I know nothing about?'

'Then if it bothers you so much it's time you did.' She looked at him seriously. 'Jeff, you're wasting yourself. You can't stay a booking-office clerk for the rest of your life.' With sudden insight she smiled. 'You're eating your-self up with self-pity because you're getting nowhere, just as I was eating myself up with hate because the world wasn't just as I wanted it. Go out and find out how our people are living. You've plenty of time when you're off duty. All you do is to sit here and wait until I come home.'

What she said was true, but she didn't know it was only half the truth. She didn't understand the very real fear of meeting someone he knew because she no longer cared if she ran into an old friend. She was living with a man, so what? It was her own business and she wasn't on her uppers any longer. She'd got a decent job and she knew she could keep it and held her head high.

Jeff slumped in his chair, the picture of dejection. Anne went and knelt by his side, putting her arms round him and resting her head against his shoulder.

'Jeff, you've never told me anything about your people any more than I have said anything about mine. I know you must have a wife. Are you afraid she won't divorce you?'

It was so pathetically far from the truth. Now was the time to say that he was afraid she would but how could he with Anne leaning so trustingly against him? He put his arms round her gently. If only she would meet someone else, someone younger and free to marry her.

'No, Anne, it's not quite like that. I don't want to hurt her. She's been a wonderful wife and there are three children.' Again it was only part of the truth.

'I see.' Anne pressed a little closer. For the first time real doubts began to pour in and the pain caught at her, tearing her in pieces. Now she knew why he had said so little. He didn't want to hurt his wife! Dear God, he probably wanted to go back to her. The pain grew worse and she had an insane longing to hurt him as she was being hurt. Tell him that he had seduced her out of his own need and without love. Then she knew she couldn't, even if it was true, and it couldn't be, Jeff wasn't like that! Wasn't he? How did she know? In those moments Anne came into her own, knew her own strength of character, knew that she would go on loving and doing what she could whatever happened. Perhaps out of this would come something far bigger if she only had the courage to face what was in between. She clung a little closer, not daring to look up in case he should see the pain in her tear-filled eyes and the sudden fear that made all her nerves jangle. After a few moments, when she knew she could speak with no tremble in her voice, she gave a small chuckle.

'It's all right, Jeff, don't worry about it. It will work out in the end. But you can't go on drifting, you've got to do something. Find out about people. Even if you don't want to write do something if it is only to talk and encourage. Don't shut yourself away. If you go out you may soon want to write again.'

During the next few days she was insistent. She almost drove him out of the flat but it didn't work. In a short time he would be back again looking completely lost. He was even more loving and at night he clung to her like a child in need of its mother's arms. Their love-making had taken on a new passion and at times she wondered if she was making a mountain out of a molehill and he was merely afraid of hurting his wife. Which of them did he want? If only she knew. She was bewildered, but in her knowledge of his need of her, her love grew stronger and deeper. She stopped caring if he loved her. Her job was to love him and during those weeks she thought more and more of Lydia. Lydia whom she had hated but who had shown her father such devotion. But Lydia had a man who had made something of his life. A man from whom she had inherited a firmness of purpose if not his brain.

If only Jeff would do something, if only she could inspire him, give him some of her force. Then whatever happened in the future it would have been worth while.

There were four other flats in the house, all occupied by

coloured families. If they passed on the stairs they murmured polite good-days and that was all and she knew she and Jeff had the reputation of being snobs. Ever since they had lived there she had worn a wedding ring except at work, when she slipped it into her handbag until she was on the way home again. Whether anyone knew their name or if they were really married she hadn't the faintest idea, but she knew they didn't care either way. She only wore the ring because it seemed the thing to do.

On Sundays, if Jeff was off duty and when the weather was fine, they took sandwiches and went out for the day. Jeff would read avidly, as if that was all he wanted to do, and Anne had taken to knitting, which was an entirely new pastime and to her pride she was getting on well. On a beautiful day towards the end of September they went to Hampstead Heath. Jeff had his eyes in a book most of the day. Every now and again, as if conscious that he should be doing something to entertain her, he teased her about the knitting, telling her that if she was not careful she would get fat with sitting so long. Anne had laughed, knowing that was the last thing she need worry about. It had been a peaceful day. The smell of grass, the leaves beginning to change colour, the noise of children playing, the bark of a dog and the singing of the birds had entered into her soul and Jeff seemed quietly contented.

On the way to the bus-stop Jeff took her basket from her, pushed his book inside and then took her hand in his.

'It's been a lovely day, Anne. Thank you for everything.'

She looked at him in sudden wonder, not quite sure what he meant.

'I mean thank you for being what you are. Accepting me as I am. There are times when I wonder what good I am to anyone. No use to my wife and children, I've done nothing I set out to do, I live with you and don't even keep you

106

and you never complain even when I am in a filthy mood. You should be out enjoying yourself with a crowd of young people instead of tying yourself to a man years older and with no prospects.'

'Oh, for heaven's sake, shut up. It's my business that I live with you. I don't think you even wanted to in the first place. I forced the issue after that first night, didn't I? I was so damn sure you wanted it that way.'

If he could have blushed he would. 'You're beginning to know me too well for my comfort. You would never have forced the issue, as you put it, if I hadn't been such an out-and-out heel.' He paused. 'Anne, I never meant to seduce you. It happened without any intention on my part. Even now I can hardly believe it.'

'Forget it. What is done is done. I'm not complaining and I could have smacked your face which, I'm dead certain, would have stopped you. You can hardly say I put up a struggle!' She giggled.

'Anne, I haven't been reading as much as you thought.'

'I'm not quite daft. I noticed how long it took for you to turn a page.'

'I was thinking. Anne, we can't go on like this. I know that now. I'll write and tell my wife. I still have most of the money left from those first articles. I'll send it to her. She'll be hurt, but I think she'll understand and give me a divorce.'

Anne walked on, not looking at him. 'Wait a little while, Jeff. Think carefully before you do anything, but you've made me very proud. I began to think you would never do anything definite.'

She had no idea why she should try to stop him. There was no reason in it, for it was the thing she wanted most in the world. It was just an inner voice which said, 'Wait, wait!'

He held her hand a little tighter. How could she ever know how much his decision cost him, but, please God, he would never let her find out. Lucy's letters were getting fewer and fewer and he was sure she knew something was wrong. It could not go on for ever and there was no point in going back. He would have no earthly chance there. If he had done something here, made something of his life, but to go home with nothing at the back of him, not even occasional writing to his credit, what hope was there? Not only that, his pride wouldn't let him. Go home with his tail between his legs like a whipped cur? Never! No, better accept the situation as it was and tell the truth. Anne and he would do the best they could with their lives and he would try to make her happy.

It had turned chilly by the time they reached their own road.

'Autumn is here already,' said Anne. 'I don't mind the winter. It's cosy to sit in a warm room and toast your feet in front of the fire.' It was seldom that Anne had any yearning for warm sea and bright sunshine. In fact she was beginning to think of England as her permanent home. There were times when she thought she would like to see her father and tell him what a fool she had been. She would like to see the rest of the family again, particularly Colin and Michael—how they must have grown! She wondered if she could bring herself to apologise to Lydia for the out-and-out little devil she had been. But she didn't want to go back home for good. That was for sure.

As they turned the corner they heard screams and shouts and saw a crowd gathering a few yards from their own door.

Jeff gave the basket to Anne and, telling her to stay where she was, joined the crowd. A coloured man lay in the gutter, a trickle of blood dripped down one cheek, a burly policeman was bending over him.

'Get up and come quietly or you'll be in for more trouble.'

'I've done nothing, I tell you, nothing.'

A big coloured woman pushed forward, screaming hysterically.

'It's my man. What you hit him for? He's done nothing.' A child clung to her skirts, sobbing. The woman caught the policeman's arm and hung on to it.

'He assaulted a white man and then resisted arrest.' The policeman tried to to shake her off, but she clung like a limpet and another woman shouted abuse. The man in the gutter got slowly to his feet.

'He wouldn't hurt anyone!' The woman was frantic with rage and fear.

'He'd better tell that at the station.' The policeman had now shaken himself free from her clutching hands and grabbed the man by the arm. 'Come on.'

The crowd was mainly coloured and mainly antagonistic. A flashily dressed man was urging them on from the outskirts with muttered remarks: 'Policemen are all the same. If it was a white man he'd let him go.'

'Joe wouldn't hurt anyone,' shouted another man. 'He'd just been out for a drink, that's all.'

Suddenly the woman began to fight. She hit the policeman in the stomach and kicked him viciously. The man called Joe caught hold of her. 'Stop it, Carrie, stop it. You won't do any good. I'd better go with him.'

Carrie was past listening to anyone. She continued to scratch and kick, her voice raised in protest. The flashily dressed man was urging the crowd on, but it was done quietly and had Jeff not been close to him he might not have realised what was happening, but he knew how quickly a crowd can be spurred on to violence and he was afraid for the consequences. He elbowed his way to the centre then, taking the woman's arm, spoke gently.

'Come along, woman, this doesn't help your man at all. If he has done nothing it will be sorted out at the station.'

The woman turned on him in fury. 'What do you know about it, Mr. Clever. You don't know nothing about us. Don't want to know.'

No, thought Jeff, I know nothing, but now is the time to find out. The crowd was now ready to turn on him for no particular reason except that any crowd is unpredictable. Several fights broke out.

'White man's boy!' shouted someone.

The policeman blew his whistle. The crowd thinned miraculously apart from those who were fighting and too incensed to know what was going on or what they were fighting about. More policemen appeared from either end of the street and, seeing the rumpus, more whistles blew. The woman was still fighting and struggling while the man was trying to stop her. The child was screaming in terror and then Anne was there, gathering the child up in her arms. It seemed to Jeff that a miracle had been performed, for suddenly it was quiet. One policeman had a couple of men in a firm grip and the others were standing at their distance, watching with sullen faces while the police watched with faces like granite. A fat white woman stood on her doorstep, arms crossed on her big breasts. She grinned and muttered, 'Black scum!' Then she spat. A coloured woman glared at her and spat back.

'Go home, niggers!' The words were shouted from an upper window.

A group of coloured men and women gathered closer together, their faces ugly with rage, and Jeff thought there would be more trouble. It was then that he raised his voice.

'Don't be foolish. You won't do any good by fighting. Only make more trouble for everyone and give people the chance to say you are no better than animals. Go to your homes and be sensible.'

'White men's pet!' The words were screamed at him.

'I'm no one's pet. I work for my living, the same as you. I want to see common sense, that's all. For your own sakes.'

The woman had stopped fighting and was now sobbing loudly. Two police cars came round the corner.

'Come on, all of you!'

'Can't you let the woman go, officer? She has a child.'

'Child! I've got four and much you care.' She turned on Jeff angrily. 'What do you care about anyone but your fancy woman!'

'Let her go? Not likely after the way she tried to stop me arresting her husband. The best thing you can do is to mind your own business.'

'This is my business. They are my people.'

'Then it's a pity you don't stop them making a nuisance of themselves.' It was not the words so much as the vicious tone that startled Jeff. Here was a man with a real chip, not the type of policeman to be patrolling a district like this.

'Let's get them to the station, Tom, we'll sort it out there.' It was a big officer with a quiet voice.

'May I come?' Jeff asked, and the officer nodded.

Jeff turned to Anne. 'Find out about the other children and see what you can do. ' The child was still in her arms and sobbing noisily on her shoulder. She smiled, patting the child's back gently.

At the station the sergeant looked at them with ex-pressionless face.

'What's the charge?'

'This man got into an argument down Coldharbour Lane. Then he knocked the man down and ran.'

'What happened to the man he knocked down?'

'I left him with Parker and gave chase to this man.'

The sergeant looked at Joe. 'What have you to say?'

Joe opened big, black and very frightened eyes. 'I wasn't even there.'

'Then why were you running?'

'I'd just been for a drink and was walking home when a man ran by me. He turned down another street and the policeman came up and caught hold of me and I pulled away and ran.'

'If you hadn't done anything why run?'

'I said I hadn't, but he didn't believe me, so I ran.'

'He's the man all right. I know by his clothes, but he was wearing a cap when I first saw him. Must have lost it or thrown it away to try and fool me.'

Joe was wearing a pair of ordinary black trousers and a dark blue windcheater. He muttered something about never wearing a cap.

'And the woman?'

Carrie was quiet enough now, but the tears were pouring down her face.

'Tried to stop me arresting him. Fought like a wild cat and told him to run.'

'And the other two?'

'Just brawling among themselves. They didn't interfere with me.' The constable looked at them with ill-concealed contempt.

'Just put them in the cells to quieten them down. Breach of the peace.' He called for a woman police officer and asked her to take the woman away. 'Give her a cup of tea,' he added, and Jeff was thankful for some show of humanity.

The phone rang and the sergeant picked it up. After a few minutes he said, 'O.K., Parker.'

'The man is in hospital and badly injured. Broken jaw and fractured skull. On the danger list. If you are the man responsible you're in for real trouble.'

'I didn't hurt anyone, I swear it.' Joe was plainly terrified.

'Take him away.' Then the sergeant looked at Jeff. 'Now what are you doing here?'

'I live a few doors down and thought it would be a good idea to come along.'

'To see fair play, I suppose.' The sergeant looked annoyed.

'Not exactly. Just because they are my people and I thought I might be of help. Now I am not so sure. For instance, I was there all the time the woman was and I never heard her tell the man to run.'

'Oh, you didn't! Well, you can tell that to the magistrate in the morning. I'm charging this man with assault and you'd better go home. Ten o'clock if you want to be there.'

There was a group of men standing at the corner of Telston Road as Jeff turned into it. Among them was the flashily dressed man. He was talking in low but forcible tones. A born trouble-maker.

'What have the white men ever done for us?' he was asking. 'They kept us poor at home and they are keeping us poor here. It's done to keep us under. All we're good for are the jobs white men won't do. Trumped up charges against us if we open our mouths. Get us so scared we're afraid to move. We're no better than slaves.' There was a murmur of agreement. Jeff stopped.

'You won't make things better by listening to such talk.' He looked the trouble-maker straight in the eye. 'All you want is to stir up trouble. Why? For your own benefit, I'll bet.'

The man glared at him. 'You keep out of this and go lick the boots of your white masters. Let them pat you on the head for being good, man. What have you done to make things better?'

'Nothing, but I won't make them worse. I notice you didn't offer to go to the station and see if there was something you could do. You got out of the way as soon as more police arrived and made sure you kept out of the way. Perhaps they know you!'

'He's right,' said one of the men. 'We won't do any good by talking, but look, man, Joe's a good chap and couldn't hurt anyone. That policeman's got his knife into us. I know him.'

'Then we'll hope British justice will do something. You've come to England to get work you couldn't get at home. I've done the same. Let's do our best to be good citizens and I'll do what I can for Joe and his family.' The flashily dress man got into a new Hillman and drove away. Jeff laughed. 'Whatever he says about being kept under he seems to be doing pretty well for himself. I wouldn't mind having his car.'

The others laughed with him. He had made a point, however small.

When he got to the flat Anne had the four children with her and was telling them a story. How many facets were there to Anne? he wondered. To see her with children was a revelation. He had never thought of her as liking children, and yet, seeing her now, he knew she would be a happy, loving and competent mother. She should have children.

'I've given them their supper and I'll take them back to their place now.' Anne smiled. 'I've told them their mummy will be back tomorrow. I'll stay with them tonight, Jeff, and ring the surgery in the morning. I can go to work as soon as their mother is back.

'I'm going to the magistrates' court. I think it's a case of mistaken identity.' He went with her to Joe and Carrie's home. There were only two rooms with a cooker on the landing and the furniture was in its last stages. The whole house seemed teeming with people and there was a damp, musty smell pervading the whole place. He made an effort not to wrinkle his nose. Anne looked at him with something like amusement.

'Never been to a house like this, Jeff, have you? I've lived in them. You're learning, fast.'

He waited until the children were asleep and told her exactly what had happened.

'Their mother won't be home until after the magistrates' court, anyhow, and goodness knows what will happen to Joe if they don't believe his story and he can't prove he wasn't there.'

'Do you believe him?'

'Yes, in spite of the fact that taking to his heels and resisting arrest makes him look guilty. I think he was just too scared to use his head. He says he just went to have a drink, so I'd better find out at which pub. Somebody might remember him although he's one of those insignificant little men who possibly slipped into a pub, had a drink and out again without speaking to a soul. It's worth trying. I wonder why the sergeant didn't ask him which pub?' Jeff was looking terribly distressed and Anne's heart went out to him.

'It's no good you taking it so much to heart. By the look of things here they're pretty shiftless.'

'How do you know if they are shiftless or if circumstances have just been against them? How do either of us know anything? We've been cooped up in our own little world and haven't cared a damn about anyone else.' He turned on Anne angrily.

'All right, Jeff, we've done nothing and know nothing but working yourself into a temper with me won't help. Go home and sleep. I'll look after the children and you'll feel better in the morning.'

He wondered if he would ever feel better. What use was he to anyone?

7

Jeff scarcely slept. He lay down for a while and then got up and paced the floor. Anne and Lucy had slipped out of his mind. He could only think of Joe and Carrie and the plight they would be in if Joe was sent for trial, let alone convicted. But it was the children that worried him most. The docile way they had submitted to Anne's care, the fear in their big dark eyes. How could you expect children to grow into normal citizens in this atmosphere of antagonism and hatred? How did they get on at school? Did this feeling penetrate even there? He didn't know but suddenly he was determined to find out. Thought of himself and his own problems fell away in this far greater one. He walked up and down, up and down, scourging himself for his past lack of interest, for the way he had drifted. Neither Anne nor Lucy existed in this moment. It was only his fellow countrymen that mattered.

In the morning he went in to see how Anne and the children were and promised he would telephone the surgery and tell them she would do her best to be in in the afternoon.

'It's the first time I've stayed away so I don't suppose they will be too annoyed.' Anne was full of smiles. 'They're nice kids. I've packed the two older ones off to school although they didn't want to go.'

'Why not?' He spoke sharply.

'Because they wanted to wait until their mother came home.'

'Is that the only reason?'

'As far as I could tell and perfectly natural where kids are concerned. Don't start looking for trouble, Jeff.'

When he left she knew he had scarcely seen her.

On the way to the court he rang the *Meteor* and asked for Gordon Robertson. It took several minutes to get through to him and he began to get nervous for fear he would be late.

'Hullo, Jeff, what's been happening to you? Long time since we've seen anything of yours.

'I know but I've a story and I want to know if you are interested.' Briefly he outlined it.

'We've got a man covering that, but if you can write it up, well, not just a report, we'd be interested. But be quick. No sense in waiting until it gets cold.'

'I'll do that.'

When he reached the court he was horrified to hear that the man who had been assaulted was dead. Things looked bad for Joe and Jeff had no idea which pub he had been in to have that drink. No one he had asked had been with him.

Thomson, the man who had arrested him, said he had been walking along the street and near the end of his beat when he saw the prisoner strike the man. It was a terrific blow and the man fell like a log, then the prisoner began to run. Constable Parker was coming from the opposite direction. He shouted to him to take care of the injured man and gave chase to the prisoner. He chased him for some distance and then the man turned into a side road and when he caught up with him he was no longer running but pretending he knew nothing about it and said a man had just passed him and turned into a nearby street.

The magistrate looked at him closely. 'So that for a few moments you lost sight of the man you were chasing?'

'Moments only, sir.'

'But in that time he might have dodged down another street?'

'Quite impossible, sir. I'm quick on my feet.'

'And suppose the other man was quicker? Were you out of breath by the time you caught him?'

There was a pause. 'Just a little, sir.'

'And the prisoner, he must have been even more out of breath. He doesn't look as fit as you.'

There was an even longer pause. 'I didn't notice, sir.'

'Why are you so sure this is the man?'

'The clothes, sir.'

'Very ordinary clothes, I may say. I understand he was wearing a cap when you saw him hit the man. What happened to that?'

'He probably threw it away.'

'That is possible. A pity no one attempted to find it.'

Constable Parker was called.

'You saw the incident and can identify the prisoner?'

'I saw the incident but I can't identify the prisoner.'

There was a gasp in court.

'You mean you didn't see him closely enough?'

'No, sir, I mean that I think the man was bigger. I didn't see him clearly, but he moved quickly, like a boxer and his shoulders were hunched. I don't think that is the man.'

The doctor who had attended the dead man was called. He said the blow had been given with tremendous strength and the man's jaw broken and he had hit his head on the kerb in falling. He doubted if the man in the dock could have struck such a blow without damaging his hand. Joe held out his hands and there was not a mark. The case was dismissed with a remark by the magistrate of the danger of mistaken identity which, in this case, had allowed a man, guilty of a crime, to escape.

The fact that he had done nothing made Jeff feel inadequate. Outside the court a youngish man accosted him.

'You're Jeff Anderson, aren't you?' He grinned. 'Robertson told me to keep an eye open for you. I'm Gregory. Wondering why the magistrate was so stiff on Thomson, aren't you, when they do their best to let the police down easy when they've made a mistake?'

'He didn't seem to mince matters.'

'No, and if you'll come and have a cup of coffee I'll tell you why. Robertson told me I was to give you anything which might help.'

Over a cup of coffee they talked.

'The business with Thomson goes back a couple of years and I've a feeling he is heading for a fall. He has it in for West Indians. There isn't any doubt about it. He's becoming a menace and the sooner they move him from this manor the better for his sake and everyone else. He's doing his best to promote trouble and I've a feeling that someone will get nasty and beat him up before long. If he wasn't a member of the force I've a feeling he would be one of the "Keep Britain White" brigade. It's not a nice state of affairs and some of his own chaps are getting fed up. It's making things hard on them. This is the second case of mistaken identity in six months on his part. It's extra bad in this one because it is manslaughter at least and they'll be lucky if they catch the man, now.'

'Thanks for telling me about it. I'll go home and do some work. I'm not on duty until late.'

'What are you doing now? It's a long time since I've seen your name in print.'

Jeff suddenly smiled. 'I'm a booking-office clerk and it's a long time since I've written anything. Time I remedied that.'

He had hardly left the café when he felt a hand on his shoulder.

'Jeff, by all that's wonderful!'

George Masters, the one man he would have avoided if possible, and yet, seeing him, hearing his voice, a warmth of boyhoood feeling flowed through him.

'I didn't even know you were in England, but I'm a damn bad correspondent. I intended to write when I left Birmingham but I put it off and put it off. I'm in partnership near here now and we must meet and have a long yarn. I can't stop as I've an appointment and I'm already late but we've got to catch up on things, man. Are Lucy and the children with you?'

Jeff shook his head. The unexpectedness of the meeting, the friendship in the dark eyes behind the thick lenses, took him by storm. To talk to George, to recapture some of the past, was suddenly all important. He accepted an invitation to dinner for two days later. He wanted to say, 'Don't ask anyone else, George, I'd rather just have your company,' but he hadn't the courage.

Anne was not in the flat and he did not even wonder if she had gone to work. For the first time in months he got out his typewriter. He could put in two hours before he went to work. Perhaps it was Gregory's story, perhaps it was the scene last night or in the court this morning, or even the meeting with George but the words came easily, fiery but unbiased, questioning rather than stating facts. He told the story of Joe and Carrie simply with no attempt to make them other than what they were. He finished the article, retyped it, put it in an envelope and posted it on his way to work.

Anne was asleep when he came home. He washed and undressed quietly and got into bed. She didn't move. He looked at her compassionately. Now that he felt he could write again, or at least try, some of his frustration had left him. Now he could look at her and make some sort of plans for the future. He thought of their first meeting, the first time he had taken her and remembered the strange attraction mingled with dislike. Now he loved her for many things, for her strength of character which made her get what she wanted, for the way she loved him, for her unexpected efficiency. He loved her passionately but not as he loved Lucy, with an abiding love which, he knew now, was the best that was in him. To no other woman could he give that love and yet he knew that he had given up his right to her. But there was the future and something must be done about it.

In the morning he told her he had written the article and sent it off and her smile was warm and proud. He told her about George and that he was having dinner with him on the following evening. She said nothing but he saw a shadow flicker across her face and knew she was feeling shut out, knew he did not want her to meet George on account of Lucy and his feeling of shame was a physical ache.

'There is nothing like coffee to put fresh life into you.' He was talking for the sake of talking because he couldn't bear her silence. 'When I was living with Doris and Reg it was the one thing I missed. Tea never seems to start the day right.'

'And today it is starting right?'

'I hope so.'

She told him she wouldn't be home until late because she was meeting Rosie and he felt a rush of relief. He could write all the evening.

On Wednesday he went to see George and there was no one else in the small, bachelor flat.

'Thought it would be more pleasant to be on our own. It's so long since we've seen each other and we can have a good natter.'

They talked over a meal prepared by George, talked about conditions at home and in England but of nothing personal. It was not until afterwards, when they were sitting over a glass of whiskey, that George asked what he was doing, whether Lucy and the children would be joining him soon. Jeff stumbled over his words, tried to make everything seem right, but it was hopeless. He and George had known each other too long, knew each other's stature. They had drifted apart, they hadn't bothered to write, but now they were together the old friendship, the old understanding was back and closer than it had been for years. It might only have been yesterday when they were together. The whole story came out slowly, painfully, and George listened. He sat utterly still, a man who was accustomed to listening to troubles both mental and physical.

'So,' Jeff muttered, 'I've got to do something, but what? I've enough money still to take me home and I can put my tail between my legs and go. Back to what? No job, no prospects. Neither can I go back to Lucy and live a lie. And what about Anne? The other day I had made up my mind to write to Lucy, to tell her all about it and ask for a divorce, but in that, like everything else, I dithered, waiting for a solution that would hurt nobody.'

'Whatever you do, Jeff, you are going to hurt someone, if only yourself. By the look of you you've been doing that for a long time. The last time I saw you you held your head high, you don't any longer. What about the book you were going to write, the things you were going to do? It seems to me that just a few set backs and you sat on your fanny and waited. Did you think the mountain would come to you? How many other writers have had their work rejected and still managed to make good in the end but they got on with it. You would never have started again without this latest incident. I suppose if this or your next is turned down you will again wait for something to turn up. Wallowing in your own midden and after a while developing an outsize chip on your shoulder. That is what worries me about our own people. All right, we often get a raw deal but what do we do about it? Complain! Do we ever try to climb out of the rut gracefully? A few do but a lot don't even try. Some make it and when they do they swagger. And when some make the grade sensibly, what happens, a whole crowd of West Indians promptly get it into their thick skulls that they have done it by licking the boots of the white man. To be accepted by white people seems to mean something dirty by some of our own.'

Jeff looked at him questioningly.

'I'm not meaning me.' George laughed. 'For some reason or other doctors are sacrosanct. Don't ask me why, I wouldn't know but when you are a doctor you see and hear a great many things. Envy, hatred and malice gnawing at men's vitals. Doing more harm than a great cancer in their stomachs. You see the tragedy and the comedy that is life.'

'The funny thing is,' he went on, 'that life is seldom fair.

123

I've been in England long enough to know it isn't only the black man that suffers under it. You need to be a doctor to see it. I know one woman who has two children, both crippled from birth and, as if that was not enough, her husband died suddenly. She copes, how I don't know but I doubt if she ever has a decent meal herself. The best she can manage goes to the children. I could tell you a hundred cases of the unfairness of life.'

'It sounds as if you should have been the writer.'

'No, I've neither the time nor the inclination. What I do hate is to see a man who has talent throwing it away. You should have brought Lucy and the children with you.'

'And let them go short because I couldn't get the right job? Let them live in poky rooms when they've always been used to a reasonable degree of comfort?'

'Better than depriving them of the love and comfort of a husband and father. Didn't you marry for better or worse? Lucy would have coped.'

'In heaven's name, George, what am I going to do?'

'That, Jeff, is your business and nobody can answer for you. You have to work out your own salvation.' Suddenly George glared at him. 'Good Good, man, haven't you anything left of what you used to be? Haven't you the courage to make up your own mind or do you want me to tell you what to do and then you can evade the blame if it doesn't turn out right?'

Jeff was startled at the anger in his voice.

'There is only one thing I can tell you to do—work! Work until you drop if necessary. Go out and meet people, find out how they live and you'll find a great many with far worse problems than you have. All right, you'll probably meet someone who knows you just as you did me and it may hurt your pride to admit that Jeff Anderson is now a booking clerk who writes sometimes. You must have spent most of your time indoors or I would have bumped into you before this. I've a patient or two in your road. Somebody may write and tell Lucy about your girl friend. That's just too bad, but if you really want to do something with your future, whether with this girl or Lucy, you can't just sit on your backside and do nothing but be sorry for yourself. I hate waste of any kind.'

The bluntness of his words, the emphasis in his voice, was like a blow in the stomach.

'You think I've been an indolent fool?' The question was both bitter and ashamed.

'Yes, I'm afraid I do, but that's not exactly damning.' George gave a broad smile. 'Aren't we all indolent fools at times?'

'I don't know whether you've been a fool, George, but indolent, never. You drove yourself on and on when everything seemed stacked against you.'

'Partly a nasty disposition which made me fight tooth and nail to prove that a barefoot boy with no background whatever could be someone. You know, Jeff, I have a great deal to thank your father for. He helped and encouraged me, gave me extra lessons in his small amount of spare time and hustled me though those first exams. The later ones I worked for when sometimes I was dropping with sleep because I was determined to make something of myself for the girl I loved. It will be hard luck on your father if his only son falls by the wayside while the barefoot boy he helped has made good.'

'But you've never married, George.'

'No, by the time I'd got through those exams you were engaged to the only girl I've ever wanted to marry.'

'I never knew.'

'There are many things you have never known. Other people's hearts, for instance. It's time you did a bit of learn-

125

ing.' He filled his pipe carefully. 'I was always fond of you, Jeff, but you've no idea how I envied you. Your parents, your home, and, later, Lucy and the children. Envy is a bad thing to go to bed with and, thank God, my work has driven it out of my system.'

'You haven't any reason to envy me now.'

'I know and it doesn't give me much satisfaction and is a pity for you.'

Jeff rose slowly to his feet and looked down at the small, slight, insignificant figure sitting so quietly in the big arm-chair. Dear God, how right George was. He had started with nothing, a child reared in poverty, not even good looks or physique to help him and he had made something of his life. He was overwhelmed with shame, a shame that seemed to live with him perpetually these days. And shame was as bad a bedfellow as envy.

'O.K., George, you've made your point. Somehow I'll sort things out however hard. Will you put up with me again at some time? When I've made up my own mind!'

'Even if I hated the sight of you I would for your father's sake but I still remember you standing between me and a crowd of big boys who were going to teach me a lesson for my colossal cheek. You were a nice kid, Jeff, and if you weren't basically decent you wouldn't be so damn worried.'

Jeff went home feeling far more chastened than in the days when his father had scolded him for not working harder. Somehow he must make good. No more shilly-shallying. His spare time must be spent in finding out more about his own people and he must make time to write.

Anne was not in. He had no idea where she was as she had said nothing about going out. At first he was flooded with a sense of freedom. He was alone in the flat, had no need to pretend in any way. He could write without the

126

feeling that Anne was watching him with either love or anxiety. It was still early, not yet ten-thirty. This was not the time to write factual articles. He did not know enough of what was going on around him but he could and would start that book. He had never written fiction before and he struggled desperately for the right theme. Could he base some of it on the story of Carrie and Joe? He could try and on his next day off he would do his best to come out of his shell and make friends with some of his neighbours. He typed frantically for an hour and covered sheet after sheet. Then he read them through, tore the last two up and started again. When he looked at the clock it was nearly midnight and Anne had not come home. Where could she be?

It was another half-hour before she opened the door and saw him sitting at his typewriter. For a half an hour he had been consumed with anxiety and now, seeing her quick smile, he was furious.

'Why didn't you tell me you were going out? I had no idea where you were. Anything could have happened. I've been worried crazy.' The fact that he had worked for well over an hour without giving her a thought was forgotten. She had no right to go out without telling him.

'I didn't think you would be back until God knows when. You said you were going to see this George, who is an old friend and obviously I wasn't needed, so I went out with a friend, too.'

'You could have told me.'

'I didn't know until this afternoon and then I couldn't get hold of you.' Anne, too, was angry, partly because she was hurt that he had not asked her to go with him although she knew in her heart that George must be someone who knew his wife. It was one of the things she must put up with, but it didn't make the hurt any the less. That she had been out with Ted made it worse, for how could she tell Jeff? Had it been anyone else it would not have mattered, but it had been that light kiss Ted had given her that had brought things to a head between her and Jeff. He would not understand her meeting him again. She felt disloyal, although the evening had been innocuous enough.

She wondered why she had been such a fool as to tell him not to write to his wife yet when she wanted to be married, wanted to wear a wedding ring honestly, wanted to have Jeff introduce her to his friends as his wife. Being a backstreet wife was beginning to hurt more than she would have thought possible. She knew Jeff loved her, but did he love her enough? She was afraid that later he would regret it, although she didn't know why the fear haunted her. Jeff's angry eyes brought her to her senses. They mustn't quarrel. It was a waste of time. She went and knelt quietly by his side and put her arms round him.

'I'm sorry, Jeff. I didn't mean to worry you, but honestly I thought you might be very late and the flat seems empty without you. Did you have a nice time?'

He capitulated, mainly because he knew he had scarcely given her a thought while he was working and had even been pleased when he came home to the empty flat.

'Not particularly. I hadn't seen George for years and things have changed.' He laughed. 'I have gone down in the social scale and he has gone up. He also gave me a well-deserved lecture for the good of my soul. It must have done some good as you see by the amount of typing I've done.'

'More articles, Jeff?'

'No, I'm going to have a struggle with the book I always said I would write. If it turns out to be no good at least I will have made an effort.'

'I'm glad. I've always wanted you to write again.'

'Even if it means no time to take you out, no going off to the pictures and no sunny days on Hampstead Heath?'

'Even if it means that although it's a bit late in the year for days on the Heath!'

Even if it means giving up your job, she thought, and living on what I earn. But that was something she couldn't suggest yet. Not until Jeff was more sure of himself, but there was nothing she wouldn't do for him, nothing.

8

By the end of the week Jeff was overwrought and completely exhausted. He had written every available moment, was convinced that everything he had written was useless and had snapped at Anne on any and every occasion. As if that was not enough he had had no word from home for more than three weeks. He had reached the stage in which when he did have a letter from Lucy he was churned up inside with conscience and when he didn't he was consumed with anxiety. None of it made sense. That his own letters home were brief and little more than friendly worried him even more but how could he write and say how much he missed Lucy and the children when he was living with Anne and sometimes forgetting all about them for days? Jeff was not a natural adulterer. He had been brought up too strictly and had too strong a conscience. He felt just as guilty to Anne as he did to Lucy and because of it Anne suffered. Mentally he turned this way and that like a rat in a cage and with no knowledge of how to gain his

129

freedom. There were times when he almost hated both women and others when he was aching with tenderness. But although he was wearing himself out the writing was an escape.

His own pent-up emotions were going down on paper but try as he would the men and women were no more than pasteboard and he could feel it. He suffered with them, feeling their agony of frustration, tight-packed living, of bitter unhappiness, but somewhere along the line he was missing out and he didn't know where. He felt it, but would the reader? He doubted it and it was that which was wearing him out far more than the actual work. Now that he had got back to writing, wanted to write this book more than he had ever wanted anything before, he began to doubt his ability to write fiction. Factual work had been his medium and he wondered if he was capable of doing anything else. But a book, a book which had been a vague, 'I'll write one sometime,' was started and somehow he must go on. It was a burning desire, it was something that might help his people in however small a way, but the people would not come alive for him.

He walked more and now the occasional slogans painted or chalked on the walls hurt in a way they had not done before. At one time he had hardly noticed them, he had just been an onlooker. Now he was one of his own people again, feeling with them and for them. Days went by, the pile of papers grew and he was taking the minimum of sleep. Anne watched him anxiously, wondering which was worse, Jeff, slumping in a chair and idling his time away or working himself to death. It seemed he knew no happy medium and she was afraid to speak about it.

On one of his days off he went in to see Carrie. Joe had already gone to work and Carrie was cleaning house. At first she was shy and awkward, obviously feeling that here was a man of education who might not understand the napkins drying on a towel horse and the steamy atmosphere which she hated as much as anyone. Carrie missed the sunshine more than Joe. She gave Jeff a cup of coffee and apologised for keeping on working, but she said she wanted to get everything done because as soon as Joe came in she went to a cleaning job in a local office.

'We want to save some money,' she said, 'because then we may be able to buy a house and let some rooms.' She went on to tell of a friend who had done just that and now he had a smart car and two houses.

'Would you rather go home, Carrie?'

The look she gave him was eloquent. Two big tears rolled down her cheeks.

'What is there to go home to? Where would we get the money? We borrowed the fare to come. Joe didn't have a job at home for months and there was no chance for the children. Here they'll have a better education and they'll do better than us. If it wasn't for that I wouldn't stop here even for Joe. I'd get home somehow. All the rain and the cold and the streets. Sometimes I just want to lay me down on a beach in the sunshine to rest my bones. Sometimes I hate England. There's no real place here for Joe and me, but there may be for the children.'

'Why was Joe afraid of the police, Carrie? He wouldn't have run if he hadn't been scared for some reason. Had they given him cause to be afraid?' Then he thought of the night on Vauxhall Bridge when he had been tempted to run for no reason! Joe was not the type to think quickly.

Carrie looked at him with quiet eyes.

'He was afraid because he had been in a bit of trouble before and thought that would come up again. When the baby was born he hadn't any money and he took some flowers from a stall to bring me and got caught. He was let

off because it was the first time and he had a good character. One of the policemen was very good and gave him five
shillings to get something for me. Joe's just silly at times.'

Jeff smiled. The police were an astonishing body. But
weren't people generally astonishing? You never knew
how they would react to anything.

On the way towards the main road a little knot of coloured men were talking. They looked at him warily. Standing with them was the flashily dressed man he had seen
on the night of Joe's arrest. Stirring up trouble again? The
look he gave Jeff was that of brazen contempt and amusement. Jeff stopped.

'You want to mind other people's business again. I told
you before, you're a white man's dog. Beat it.'

Jeff smiled, unperturbed at the rudeness, determined to
find out what the man was up to.

'I'm just interested as to why you complain of the white
man when you seem to be doing well here. Isn't that your
car?' The shiny Hillman with the plastic flowers by the
windscreen and the mock leopard-skin seat covers was
nearby.

'What's that to do with you?'

'I just asked. If you can have a new car it means you've
got the money from somewhere. Working for the white
man or letting rooms at a wickedly high rent to your fellow
countrymen.'

'That's my business.' He clenched his fists and glared.
'We don't want you here. Get going.'

'Why don't you wait for your friends to speak? They
haven't suggested I should go. Or do you want me to go
because you are afraid I shall hear what you are talking
about?'

The narrow-brimmed trilby hat was pushed to the back
of the close-cropped hair, the narrowed eyes were vicious.

The sickly smell of cheap perfume assaulted Jeff's sensitive nostrils.

'As a matter of interest, how do you make your money? Not as these men do, by sheer hard work, I'll bet.' He looked at the man standing next to him and remembered he's seen him sweeping the main road only a couple of days before. 'Not like you do, pushing a big broom in all weather. Talk's cheap when you don't work.'

The man went to his car but he still managed to swagger. Jeff laughed and for the first time in many weeks it was a genuine, easy amusement. He turned to the men who had been silent during this passage of words.

'What does he do and what is he up to?'

'He wants us to form a union for coloured people only so that we fight for our own rights.'

'And of course you would have to pay for this and I suppose he would collect the dues?'

The men nodded. Jeff asked what they, apart from the road sweeper, did. Two were cleaners on the Underground, two on the buses and the other a dustman.

'And do you get less money than the white men who work with you?' They shook their heads. 'Then what the devil do you want another union for? You all belong to one. Were you actually thinking of joining?'

'He said that if we were sacked for something our unions would never do anything for us because we're not white but this one would. He'd got the cards ready for us.'

'And how much would you have to pay for this, supposed, safeguard?'

'Five shillings a week.'

'Man, man, have you taken leave of your senses? Have you ever heard of a meeting of this union?' They looked surprised. 'Unless I'm much mistaken he's just a trickster, trying to get money under false pretences. Do you know where he lives?'

'Not around here.'

'Of course he doesn't. I don't suppose he has ever done an honest day's work in his life. Trust your own unions until they let you down and then it will be time to do something but not in this way. Keep your money in your pockets. I don't suppose you have any to throw away. There are men like that all over the world trying to get money for nothing and if I have my way I'll catch that one sooner or later. Don't let him get rich on your money.' He stayed a bit longer to chat and then went on his way.

Human nature, he thought, is much the same anywhere. The following day he had a letter from Robertson enclosing a cheque. He put it straight in the bank but this time he had no grand ideas. It was just a bit of luck that he happened to live in the same street as Carrie and Joe. He sat down and wrote an article on the cupidity of human nature whatever colour. By now he had gathered together a good many facts and could substantiate them. He also had a longing to break Mr. Flashy but hadn't the faintest idea how to set about it. Then he went back to his book and worked until three in the morning in spite of the fact that he had to be on duty at five-thirty. When he got home that night he was too tired to eat and his eyes were swollen with fatigue. Anne was irate.

'I wanted you to start writing again, but there's no sense in killing yourself. You didn't come to bed at all last night and you haven't come straight home.'

'I went to see a man who is having trouble with his land-lord.'

'You don't do things by halves, do you? You either sit and do nothing by the hour or go completely mad and work yourself to death.'

'Oh, shut up. I don't want anything to eat. I'm going to bed.' He stripped off his clothes and left them lying on the floor and as soon as his head touched the pillow he slept. He didn't even feel Anne get into bed, didn't know she lay wakeful, afraid to move in case she disturbed him. Several times she was tempted to put her arms round him, to wake him, to ask him the question she had wanted to put the night before but had pushed to one side when she saw his exhaustion.

'Jeff,' she had wanted to say, 'I'm tired of living like this, after all. Do you love me enough to marry me if Lucy will divorce you?'

It wasn't until dawn that she fell asleep and then it was deep and dreamless and when she wakened it was to the smell of coffee and Jeff was standing by the bed with a cup and saucer in his hand. He looked perfectly refreshed. It was Anne who was exhausted.

'Sorry I was bad-tempered last night, Anne. You were right, I've been over-doing it, but last night I slept like a top and feel fine this morning.' He didn't say that he had already been up for two hours working. He had been writing rather than use his typewriter, for fear the clickety-clack should disturb her.

She sat up in bed and took the coffee from him.

'Go and fetch yours here,' she said, wondering if it would be a good time to ask him, but when he came back he was full of the fact that he was going to see a family who were in grave straits financially because they had taken on far too much hire-purchase. Instead of the personal question she intended she asked him how he was getting on with the book.

'I've written a tremendous lot, but I don't know if it is any good. Would you like to read it? You could tell me what you think of it so far.'

135

She felt a little glow inside. He wanted her opinion. Her eyes were wide and luminous.

'I wouldn't be much of a critic. You see I've never been a great reader. I read all the books I had to at school, but since I've been in England I've hardly read at all. Too full of myself, I suppose. But I'd like to read it just the same.' Whatever you asked me to do I'd do it, she thought.

On the way to work she took herself to task for being a fool. Why hadn't she talked to Jeff about themselves? He had said he would write to Lucy and she had been idiot enough to stop him. Why, why, why? But she knew the answer. Jeff still didn't know for sure what he wanted to do and she was desperately afraid, afraid that if he asked Lucy for a divorce and then regretted it he would blame her and she knew that was something she could not bear. She had begun to realise that she had been the one who had pushed things along until they were where they were now. After that first night she doubted if Jeff would have ever slept with her again had she not been so certain then that he was just as much in love with her as she with him.

That morning Rosie rang her. She had an unexpected evening off and could Anne meet her? Anne hesitated. Jeff had promised to be in by eight-thirty and she wanted to have a meal ready for him.

'Oh, Rosie, not for the evening. I'll have a cup of tea with you in the café round the corner but I can't stay long.'

Rosie was looking wonderful in a light green outfit that showed off her creamy skin and flaming hair to perfection. She greeted Anne with a rapturous smile.

'Anne, look, I've been dying to see you.' She held out her left hand and on the third finger was a ring with a small sapphire surrounded by tiny diamonds. 'Jimmy's asked me to marry him and yesterday he bought this. It's second-hand,' she spoke with her usual open-hearted candour, 'but that way the stones are good and I like old-fashioned things.'

'But, Rosie, you're so young and I thought you intended to have a good time before you settled down.'

'I know but we're not getting married for at least two years. We want to save up and buy a little house somewhere. Oh Lord, I never thought I could be so happy and to think when I first began to go around with him it was just because I liked the way he talked and I thought I could learn a bit. I wasn't a bit serious.'

They sat at a small table and Rosie grinned. 'I had intended to take you out for the evening but this is my treat anyhow.' She ordered tea and cakes, then added toast and looked at Anne critically.

'You were always thin, Anne, but I believe you're thinner. What are you doing to yourself? Don't you eat properly?'

'Of course I do. What put that into your head?'

'I don't know. You're different somehow. You're softer and warmer and you don't say beastly things any more. At one time you didn't care for anything or anybody. Now I think you do but in some funny way you seem sort of nervous. You've never asked me to your flat, Anne. You don't see me anything like as much as you used to. There is a reason, isn't there? Is it something to do with Ted? If it isn't what is it?'

Anne sat holding her cup of tea in both hands. The need to talk to someone was too great and Rosie could be trusted utterly. She told her the story of Jeff and herself much as he had told George but the difference was that she had no dividing loyalties.

Rosie's honey-gold eyes filled with tears. 'Oh, Anne, how could you be so silly and I thought you were clever and capable of looking after yourself and you always seemed to be as cool as a cucumber where men were concerned. I always thought it would be you who would do the laughing at them.'

'So did I, Rosie, but I didn't know I could love a man so that nothing mattered except making him happy and I don't really know if I am doing that. I'm not sure now whether it's me or his wife he wants and I don't think he knows himself. If I were sure of that it would be easy.'

'And suppose he does want to go back to his wife, what will you do?'

'What can I do? Just let him go, I suppose.' Her mouth tightened. 'Don't think I shall do anything daft and don't feel sorry for me. It's been worth it, every bit. And don't think I feel ashamed of myself, I don't.'

'I can't imagine you doing that.' Rosie smiled. 'But I don't want you to be unhappy and however much you love him he sounds a drip to me. For a grown man not to know what he wants is stupid.'

For a moment Anne's eyes blazed and then she laughed.

'Oh, Rosie, to you everything is straight forward. All cut and dried and neatly stowed away but it isn't like that for everyone. You're very grown up in some ways and very young in others. If you knew Jeff you might understand better. You see I think that part of the trouble is he is something like you. Got a keen sense of right and wrong. He got caught up in this because I haven't any sense of right and wrong at all. I know what I want and set out to get it and the devil take the hindermost and this time the hindermost may be me!' She smiled. 'You're a darling, Rosie, and it has done me good to talk about it. If I go to the ends of the earth I'll never forget you. I've never asked you to the flat because, although I don't care a button, I think Jeff would be uncomfortable if you gave him one of those straight looks.'

138

'Take care of yourself, Anne, and don't get any thinner or you'll disappear.'

It had done Anne good to talk. She went home feeling lighter than she had done for some time and bustled around preparing a particularly nice meal. Perhaps tonight Jeff wouldn't work so late. They'd go to bed early and find perfect happiness in each other's arms. Lately he had avoided love-making and that hurt. Once she had the meal ready she sat down with the typewritten pages. It was true that she had not read much of late, but she had a perceptive brain and after the first few pages she was engrossed in the story.

It was good, it was well written, the words flowed easily but there was something wrong. It took her some time to realise what it was and when she looked up Jeff was standing there. She hadn't even heard him come in. Without pausing to weigh her words she spoke.

'I like it, Jeff, but it's like those first articles you wrote. It's emotional without bite. The people are rather pathetic, no real spunk. Some may be like that but most of us have a touch of the devil. This woman, for instance, isn't she just that bit too patient? Wouldn't she throw the nearest saucepan at her husband when he came home drunk because life was beating him? This bit, in the second chapter, instead of crying into her pillow I think she'd blast him : I know people in books are larger than life but these are not really living. You are suffering with them but not happy with them or angry with them and life is all three. Perhaps it's because you are too gentle and nobody can really get angry with you.'

He took the pages from her hand and read them. 'You're right, Anne, that's what she should do. Perhaps you're right, too, nobody has thrown a saucepan at me.'

'Would you like me to start?' She chuckled. 'I'm perfectly capable of it and more.'

'I believe you are are and it wouldn't be a bad idea. I'm often a surly brute and I don't even look after you properly and you keep yourself. Why are you so patient?'

'Perhaps because I know you can't help yourself.' She looked at the clock. 'Now is the time to start. You said you would be in by half past eight and it's well after nine and the meal will be ruined.'

'Anne, I'm sorry, I went into the Gordons' along the road and got caught up in an argument about politics.' He put his arms round her and she rested her head against his shoulder.

'It doesn't matter, darling, you never come home drunk.' She gave a little giggle and he didn't know her eyes were full of tears, Where, she asked herself, had this all enveloping love come from?

Over their meal they talked about the book and Jeff said he wouldn't work on it tonight, it was better to forget it for a while. They went to bed early and when he took her in his arms his passion and tenderness was all she desired. She slept like a child, her head on his shoulder, and this time it was Jeff who lay awake, grateful for her love but tortured by doubts. If only he could be sure what was the right thing to do. He felt pathetically humble and knew he didn't deserve the love this girl gave him. He wanted to do the right thing, if only he knew what that was.

In the morning Anne's face was alight. All her doubts had miraculously fled and she was radiantly happy and on top of the world. Jeff did love her, without the slightest doubt. Why had she been worrying so? It was just that he wanted to break the news to Lucy gently.

9

In the next few weeks Jeff had no time to churn himself into knots about anything for he was working too hard. Robertson bought his second article and it gave him fresh hope. And then there was the book. He realised that for him fiction was a great deal harder than pure facts, but whenever it seemed the book would never be finished there was Anne. She read chapter by chapter and her own mixed personality, with the hardness and softness wound so inextricably together, saw both weakness and strength and she wasn't afraid to speak her mind. And what was more Jeff listened, instantly realising how clearly she could often see a point that escaped him. The best side of his nature came uppermost. He was unashamedly willing to learn from her. The force of her character was a spur and he knew it.

He knew he could never get Lucy out of his mind and heart, she was entrenched there too deeply. Whatever happened he would carry a load of guilt about her. There would be times when he would yearn to see her and his children and parents but he was beginning to look facts in the face. He couldn't have it all ways. And he knew he loved Anne. He knew, too, that she was giving him something Lucy had never been able to give, perhaps because she was too like him and took things as they came, accepting but not making a great effort to change them. Had she been Anne she would have somehow come to England with him, come hell or high water. Nothing would have stopped her.

Anne was a fighter in every sense of the word and she had an insight into other people in an astonishing way. She saw into them and through them. Even over Carrie and Joe she had been so right. They hadn't had much chance but they were feckless. The money they had been scraping together to put down for a house was suddenly spent on a ramshackle car which they didn't need.

'Why do they do it?' he asked Anne. 'It doesn't take Joe five minutes to walk to work and Carrie gets a bus anyhow. Where is the sense?'

Anne laughed. 'Darling, why do you let it worry you? The Carries and the Joes seldom learn. They have what they want at the moment.'

'But it's so senseless. They live in appalling conditions. They've saved so hard and now they have the car they will spend anything they might save on running it.'

'So what! They are having a wonderful time until they get fed up. You can't live other people's lives for them, nor give them common sense.'

'How right you are! Living one's own life is difficult enough without trying to live other people's.'

Anne busied herself with her cooking, not looking at him, afraid of how difficult he was finding his own life.

The book developed in a way Jeff had never intended. It was pungent, biting and, at times, passionate. When it flagged Anne would urge him to alter it, to quicken the pace, make it more forceful. Sometimes she would be deliberately cruel and tell him he was positively mawkish. For a time he would sulk and then suddenly see the funny side. During these weeks they found something between them entirely new. A flash point which would spark off both their brains. They quarrelled in a way they had never done before and they made up equally quickly. They laughed more and Jeff discovered a sense of fun he thought he had forgotten. He recaptured a boyishness that had been lost years ago. Occasionally they would take an evening and go dancing and Anne realised that he no longer tried to avoid people when he was with her. He didn't seem to care any more who knew they were living together. He didn't go to see George again.

Christmas came and went. Jeff wrote to Reg and Doris and told them he was working hard on a book but hoped to see them in the new year. He called to see Alf and Lizzie while Anne was at work. At sometime he would take her to see them but not yet. On Christmas morning Anne had insisted on going to church and after they had their dinner she refused to let him go back to the book. Afterwards he realised how right she had been. He needed that day away from everything.

'I'm glad I wasn't on duty today. Wise little monkey, aren't you?' They were sitting in front of the fire, Anne on the rug with her head on Jeff's knee. He tweaked her ear, gently. 'You knew I needed a complete break.'

'Somebody has to have a bit of sense round here. You haven't got much!'

He pulled her to her feet and slapped her backside. 'You are also a cheeky little monkey and it's time you treated me with respect.'

She giggled helplessly. 'Oh, Jeff, I do love you when you come all over lord and masterish. It makes me feel we really do belong.'

As if we really do belong, he thought, that's the rub. We should belong. She gave him so much, loved him so passionately and sometimes he felt like a cold and hungry man, warmed and fed, but giving nothing in return. As the book grew that, too, fed on her warmth and fire. During that time she was full of radiance, a light to the dark patches of his soul and he could no more have given her up than taken wings and yet he was still consumed by a sense of guilt.

It was towards the end of January. Jeff was worried. He

had heard that men had been threatened if they did not join the new union for coloured workers. One man had been badly beaten up but swore it was no more than a pub brawl. Jeff did not believe him. If only he could get the real facts but it was so difficult to get people to talk.

'It's nothing more or less than a protection racket,' he said to Anne. 'Pay up or else. I'd like to find who is at the bottom of it. That flashily dressed swine is not the main mover in it, I'll swear. He hasn't the brains. Just carries out the orders. Too, there must be some real thugs working for them. Somehow I'm going to find out.'

'Jeff, Anne looked at him in alarm. 'Do be careful.'

'Are you afraid I can't take care of myself?' He flexed his muscles and grinned.

'Of course I'm afraid. You're rather like a bull at a gate. If it is a protection racket and you interfere you'll get the worst of it. It's not your business, it's for the police.'

He took her in his arms and began to laugh. 'You really are a proper little hen, getting your feathers all ruffled before there is a hint of danger. There's nothing to be scared about.'

'Of course there is, you great big idiot. I don't want you hurt. Wasn't it bad enough to get set on by a gang of silly boys without men who are paid to beat people up!'

He took her chin in his hand and turned her face up to his. 'You know, my sweet, I don't deserve all this consideration. What on earth do I do for you?'

'Love me!' She gave him a pert grin. 'You do, don't you?'

It was the first time she had ever asked him and now he knew he couldn't deny her.

'Yes, darling, I love you.' He held her gently, possessively. 'I love you and it's time I did something about it. We

144

can't go on like this any longer. I'll write to Lucy and tell her. Sometimes I think she knows there is someone else and I'm sure she'll give me a divorce.'

Anne's eyes filled with tears. 'Jeff, are you sure? I don't want you to do anything you may regret later.'

'I'm sure, Anne, quite sure. We'll talk about the financial side. There's the house and I have the money I've earned at writing. I don't want her or the children to go short. You do understand that?'

'Of course I do. As long as you really want me nothing else matters.' It was what she had ached to hear for so long. Her cup of happiness was brimming over.

The following night Jeff was walking along the main road when, in the bright light of a shop, he saw again the flashily dressed man. This time he was not alone. A big man who stooped, who wore a cloth cap and a windcheater, was walking with him. Suddenly bells jangled in Jeff's brain and he remembered the words of the constable when Joe came up before the magistrate. A bigger man than Joe who walked with a stoop and wore a cloth cap, a man who moved like a boxer. The whole idea was ridiculous! There must be hundreds of men walking around with that description. But it was more than that. He was with Flashy. Birds of a feather. A union that urged people to join by force! Jeff was determined to find out more. Men like this could do so much damage. Help to put bigger chips on the shoulders of those who already had small ones. If he had enough information he could go to the police but he didn't know enough. He hadn't even been able to get hold of one of the 'union' cards. It was more like a secret society than anything. The men he talked to were cagey and, he was certain, scared.

He followed at a discreet distance, wanting to see if they had contacts, hoping to find where they lived. It was strange that Flashy hadn't his car with him. Wherever they were going it must be fairly close. They turned down a side street and he followed. Then down a narrow alley. But the alley was empty. Blaggs Lane, that was it. He hesitated, puzzled. He walked along cautiously, knowing something was amiss. Had they known he was following them all the time? In the darkest part of the alley a figure moved, a light was flashed in his face.

'It's him all right. Let him have it, man, teach him to mind his own business.'

The big man brought up his great fist, but Jeff was light on his feet and moved quickly, avoiding the blow and landing a heavy one on the man's jaw, although it made little impression.

If only that first blow had landed and Jeff had gone down it might have ended then and there, but Jeff's blood was up and he was a fighter. A gate opened and out of the corner of his eye Jeff saw several men coming towards him and he knew then he had been a fool. There was no chance now to cut and run. Even as he fought he knew that all the men surrounding him were not West Indians but they were all the same type. Riff-raff of dockside and back street. Scum of any city anywhere. Even in his desperate need he tried to fix their faces in his mind. There was one in particular, a white man leaning against the fence under the only light. Taking no part in the fight but smiling delightedly, as if this was the breath of life to him, watching brutality by other men but never risking his own skin. Jeff knew he was fighting for his life for that man would never have shown his face had he thought Jeff would live to tell the tale. There was a glint of steel and a sharp pain in his arm and then in his side but he fought on doing his utmost to give some punishment in exchange for what he was receiving. At last he went down, helpless against his enemies, but even then there was no respite from the vicious kicks. Black night descended and he knew no more.

Anne was walking on air. Her happiness knew no bounds. Jeff was working harder than any slave in the old days but his frustrations had vanished and he was letting her into his innermost thoughts, talking about his work as if she had every right to know, listening to her comments and obviously grateful for her understanding. He was hers in every way. Vaguely she knew that never before had he shared his work with anyone. The book was almost finished, the final chapter started. All that remained to be done then was the fair copy. She knew it was a good book, and obviously grateful for her understanding. He was hers be accepted. And now he had made up his mind about Lucy. Her heart soared. When the book was done they could straighten out their own lives and do their best to make some reparation to Lucy. In the meantime nothing mattered. She was too happy to care. It was odd that until he had begun to put out all his efforts she had never been certain, but now they were spending less time in love-making, less time together and seldom going anywhere just for pleasure, they were so much happier.

There was another reason for her happiness although she didn't want to tell Jeff until the book was finished. She was pregnant. Would Jeff be pleased? She hoped so for she wanted the baby with all the intensity of her passionate heart. Maybe it would have been better if it hadn't happened till the book was sold, but she had been care-less and that was all there was to it. Anyhow, it was early days yet. No need to tell Jeff. He was engrossed in his work and wouldn't suspect and she was feeling wonderful. No regrets whatever. Now it didn't matter if they were never married. She could help Jeff with his work, encourage and talk to him. The book had been just as thrilling to her as to him. She had lived it with him and looked forward to the next with an eagerness of a woman newborn. Where all her former energies had gone into hate now they went into love and as yet the love was as untamed as the hate. She gave no thought to Lucy or any unhappiness she would have, neither did it dawn on her that seeing her child would remind Jeff of his others.

It's Jeff, she thought, he's altered me completely. He's so good and kind and sees the best in everyone. It didn't dawn on her that Jeff had not altered her at all. She was the same forceful personality but with a different outlook. She saw people with different eyes, no longer looked for insults nor felt contempt. She loved Jeff so much and did not think that she was the stronger character.

She had seen Ted once since Christmas and told him it was better they didn't meet again.

'I'm sorry, Anne, I was an awful fool. It took me so long to know I was in love with you and then it was too late. If I'd known sooner, before you met this other man, perhaps you would have married me.'

'Perhaps I would, Ted, but it wouldn't have been a good marriage.'

'I want you to have the address of my bank, Anne. Wherever I am it will find me and if you ever need me I'll be there.'

'No, Ted, it's better not. Forget me as soon as you can and you may meet someone else before long. Someone who will love you. Marriage won't work with love on one side only.'

She watched him drive off, glad it was ended, knowing that however sad his face he would forget her, perhaps sooner than he thought. The fact that she did not want him had made him more eager to marry her and she had the sense to know it. Now she wanted no reminders of her past stupidity. She had grown up.

Tonight she had been out with Rosie for she knew Jeff would not be in until rather late. She talked about her new happiness and Rosie, child that she still was in some ways, crossed her fingers. Anne was almost too happy, she sparkled.

'As soon as the book is finished you must come and meet Jeff, I was going to ask you to bring Jimmy but perhaps you had better not.' She chuckled. 'I know you don't really approve but you are fond of me. Jimmy might be too shocked to try and understand.'

'I don't mind now you look so happy. I may even like your Jeff if he can keep you looking like you do now. It isn't so much that I disapprove but I'm afraid for you more than anything. I thought I loved Jimmy, I do love him, but not as you do your Jeff. Not enough to burn my boats and risk the future without being married. I've always thought that once you give yourself to a man before you are married he doesn't care anymore. I suppose I haven't your courage.'

'Stop worrying about me. I don't think there is anyone in the world happier than I am.'

'No, I don't think there is and I hope you'll always be as happy.' But whatever she said Rosie was worried. It seemed to her that Anne's happiness was like bright sunshine after rain, dazzling and glorious but not lasting. It was too bright. Instinctively Rosie felt there was another storm coming.

Jeff was not home when Anne got in but she wasn't worried. He had said he would be late and so often now he went out on this eager hunt to talk to people, to find out how they lived, their problems and their joys. She didn't mind that he did not want her with him now because she knew they would talk more freely when she was not there. The only one she would have liked to meet was George, whom he sometimes talked of. She knew he was no longer afraid of anyone knowing they lived together and that he intended to write to Lucy so why worry.

It wasn't until after midnight that she grew anxious. He was never as late as this except when he was on late turn. By two in the morning she was frightened. He would have told her if he was going to be as late as this for he had become more and more considerate about that. If he was delayed somewhere why didn't he phone? She made no attempt to go to bed. Reading the last chapter of the book once more she realised it would only take a few pages to finish it. It had become so much part of her that she thought she could do it herself. She wanted to but she had better not. Jeff might be angry. If only she had something to occupy her mind until he came. If she were a typist she could have started on that final copy but her typing was of the two finger variety and full of mistakes. This must be done expertly.

At three-thirty there was a knock on the door. Her heart bounded, seemed to stand still and then raced again. It wasn't Jeff for he would never have knocked. She went to the door with shaking legs and eyes wide with terror. A policeman stood there quietly, stolidly. She held on to the door and waited, saying nothing.

'Mrs. Anderson?'

She never even thought of saying yes. Just shook her head and said, 'Something has happened to Jeff. What is it?'

'May I come inside?'

She opened the door wider, but did not dare let go of its support. He saw the terror in her face and took her arm, gently leading her to a chair. She might not be Mrs.

Anderson, but he guessed the position without being told. The look on the girl's face was enough for that. Poor little devil, probably far worse than if she was his wife: No rights whatever and that must be damn hard.

'This is Mr. Anderson's flat, isn't it?'

She nodded.

'Then if you are not his wife you must be a close friend.'

She nodded again.

'Has he any relatives in England?'

Somehow she found her voice. 'No, only me. Please tell me what has happened.'

'It's an accident, miss. He's in hospital.'

'Very bad?'

'I'm afraid so.'

'Please take me to him.'

'Would you like a cup of tea first? To steady you a bit. I can make it.' The English and their eternal tea!

'No, thank you. Just take me to him.'

Jeff lay in the high, white bed. There was a nurse there and a police officer. He lay very still, a bandage round his head and another round his arm. A long tube came from a suspended bottle on the other side of the bed. She had never noticed before how dark he was. Far darker than her own soft brown.

'It wasn't an accident, was it?' She looked at the police officer. 'It was a fight.' Her voice was suddenly calm.

'What makes you say that? Has he been mixed up in fights before?'

'No, of course not. I don't really mean a fight. I think he was beaten up.'

'Have you any particular reason for thinking that? Know anyone who has a grudge against him?'

'No, but he is a writer and lately he has been making lots of inquiries.'

'Such as?'

She told the little she knew quite simply. She was even able to describe the flashily dressed man and his car. Jeff had told her so much about him.

'We can't do much until he regains consciousness. He may be able to tell us who it was then.'

She looked at Jeff's utterly still body and she ached with an agony of fear. If he ever regains consciousness, she thought. I warned him to be careful and he treated it like a joke. A doctor came into the room and put a comforting hand on her shoulder.

'Come with me, there is nothing you can do here at the moment.'

He took her to a small room and someone gave her a cup of tea but nothing registered except her fear for Jeff. Jeff, who had only wanted to help his own, who hadn't a bit of hate for anyone.

'The constable told me you are not his wife but he has no one else here. It isn't much good pretending. He's in a very bad condition. He was found about midnight and brought straight here. We would have sent for you sooner but he was in a very bad way and the first thing was to do what we could for him. He'd lost a great deal of blood and we didn't know who he was. Then a nurse went through his clothes again and in the corner of a pocket found a crumpled envelope. There was nothing inside. It should have been found sooner. Not that you could have done anything. He was in the theatre until a short time ago. Two ribs had been smashed in, apart from a stab wound in his arm and another in his side.'

'Is he going to get better?'

'Who can say? He has a strong constitution.'

'His head is bandaged, too.'

'He has a nasty wound on the back of his head.'

'I hope they catch whoever did it.' Some of the old hate came back in a surging flood. 'He wouldn't hurt a soul.'

No, he thought, not physically, but just how much are you going to be hurt?

'Will you tell me your name, please.'

'Hunter. Anne Hunter.'

'Do you know if Mr. Anderson has any relatives?' He hated asking her. 'Is he married?'

She nodded, briefly, not even caring.

'Have you his wife's address? We should get in touch with her.'

She stared at him, suddenly realising the implication. She had no rights, it was his wife who should be here. Thank goodness Jeff had said so little about Lucy, that he had never given her any indication of where she lived. Quite truthfully she answered.

'No, I know nothing about her.' Calmly and with sudden pride that lifted her words out of any trace of sordidness, 'I've been living with him for a long time and we hope to get married when he gets a divorce.'

'I see. Then there is nothing we can do to get in touch with his relatives at present?'

'No, nothing.'

That she believed her words he hadn't the slightest doubt but he wondered if it was as straightforward as she thought. He'd seen other girls with just as much faith and seen them beaten when the wife appeared on the scene. She was a beautiful girl and he could understand a man on his own falling for her. That was the damnable part of these separations. So often a marriage drifted apart. Sometimes it drew together again, sometimes it didn't, but in this case he felt a deep sympathy for the girl. He could see the pain she was suffering for this man and, after all, he didn't know what the wife was like. She could be having a thin time somewhere, but she could be enjoying herself with someone else. It wasn't his business. His job was to do his best to drag the man back to life.

'The best thing you can do is to go home. It may be hours before he regains consciousness, it may be days. He has a slight skull fracture as well as the wound on the back of his head, as if the other injuries weren't enough. I'm sure the police will take you home.'

'Can't I wait here?'

'If I thought it would do any good to you or to him I would say yes but it won't. I am going to give you a couple of pills to give you some rest. You can come back first thing in the morning.'

He took her to see Jeff once more, gave her the pills and she was taken home. The pills remained in her bag. She dare not take them because they might send for her and she wouldn't wake. She didn't bother to take off her clothes, but lay on the bed she had shared so long with Jeff and closed her eyes. She tried to hurry on the future mentally. To picture the time when he had made a perfect recovery and she would recapture the happiness she had had in the past weeks. It was no good. All she could see was Jeff's still figure. The straight nose with the flaring nostrils, the mouth that was womanish in its gentle curves. She forgot about her pregnancy. Her whole body was one great prayer to the God she had almost forgotten.

'Please, please, God, let him get better. I don't care what happens to me but let him get better. He can do so much good. Don't let him die. It would be such a waste.'

She muttered the words over and over again. At last she dropped into a fitful doze. 'Jeff, Jeff.' She murmured the name continually and when she wakened it was as if she had never slept, for instantly the knowledge of what had happened was with her. Without bothering about anything she went to the phone. No, there was no change. How long could it go on like this? she wondered. How long could she live with this tearing pain? She waited until nine and then rang the surgery. A relative had met with a bad accident and she was needed. She recognised the nurse's sympathetic voice, unaware that the agony in her own was more effective than any words could have been. Then she rang Rosie's number and asked for her. Rosie, the one person who would understand. She clung to the thought of Rosie like a drowning man to a straw.

'All right, Anne, I'll be with you as soon as I can. I know Mrs. Lowe will understand.'

It was the first time Rosie had ever asked for extra time off, and Mrs. Lowe, knowing she had a treasure, gave it gladly. In a remarkably short time she was at the flat and she never told Anne she had done a thing she had never done in her life before—taken a taxi. Anne's ravaged face wrung her heart. Only last night she had been so happy. She went with Anne to the hospital and waited for hours.

Had it not been for Rosie, Anne did not know how she would have got through the next days and Rosie thanked her lucky stars that she worked for a woman with so much heart. She had gone back that first evening for some clothes and quietly told Mrs. Lowe the whole story.

'You see,' she said, 'Anne isn't like other people. There's something big about her, something I don't understand at all, but I love her as if she were my sister. I think I always have and there's no one but me to help her, no one but me to be with her. It's not that I think she would do anything silly if he should die, but everyone needs someone to stand by, don't they?'

'Yes, Rosie, everyone needs someone to stand by them and she is lucky she has you. Stay as long as you are needed. I understand.' She looked at Rosie's tear-filled eyes and then put her arms round her and hugged her. 'It was a lucky day when you came to me. You're one of the most loyal people I know.'

Rosie insisted on Anne eating, however little, she went backwards and forwards to the hospital with her, she watched the hollows in Anne's cheeks getting deeper and her heart ached. There was nothing she could do to ease the agony, only stand by and let Anne know she loved her. And her love got through. Anne knew she was not alone and slowly became a little less frozen and began to realise there was room in her heart for more than one love. Rosie, dear, kind Rosie, for whom she had at first felt so much contempt. Rosie who could stand by a friend like a strong tree, shielding her just a little from the cold, bleak wind.

Days went by and there was still no change. The doctors began to wonder if Jeff's brain had received permanent damage. There were no letters from his home and Anne was glad because if any came she might have felt she should take them to the hospital. She hadn't looked among his papers for fear she should find one. On the second night Rosie persuaded her to take a sleeping tablet, promising faithfully she would wake her if she should be sent for.

'But I mightn't wake, whatever you did.' There was terror in Anne's voice. It was her greatest fear. That he should be taken worse and she would never get there in time.

'Don't be silly, dear, of course I should be able to wake you. You can't go on without sleep.' Then Rosie struck the right note. 'When he regains consciousness you don't want to be too ill to go to him, do you, and if you don't get some sound sleep soon that is what will happen.'

She had no conviction that Jeff would ever regain consciousness, let alone get better, but her quiet note of confidence worked. Anne took a sleeping tablet and went to bed.

10

It was a raw day in February when Anne phoned the hospital and they told her there was a slight improvement and Jeff was asking for her. She and Rosie walked the short distance and the eagerness in Anne's walk, the expectancy in her eyes, touched Rosie even more than her previous agony. There was such hope in every movement and Rosie prayed silently that all her hopes would be fulfilled. The wind whipped round the corners bitingly, but Anne didn't seem to feel it. Her heart was too full of deep gratitude. Her prayers had been answered. Jeff had turned the corner and the whole world would soon be right again. Hope bloomed like a flower, lit her eyes and parted her lips. There was something almost frightening in such sudden joy.

She went straight to his room. The nurse smiled at her. The staff were uninterested in her relationship with this man, but her devotion was such they all felt for her. Jeff was lying quite still and looked no different from what he had the day before. Anne's heart sank.

'Don't worry,' the nurse said, 'it was only a flicker but he spoke your name. It may be some time before he does it again, but you're here now and it will be good for him to have you by his side.'

Anne sat close by the bed and took his hand in hers. He didn't move. Sister came in.

'Talk to him quietly,' she said. 'It may help him to hear your voice.' She went again, but the nurse was still there.

'Jeff, darling,' she murmured, 'I'm here, it's Anne, can you hear me?'

Her eyes were on Jeff's beloved face so she didn't see

the scared look the nurse gave her. She went on talking, saying anything that came into her head, about the book, the weather, anything. Trying to reach down in the pit where he had sunk. Time went by and she still talked on but he made no response. Just as she had begun to think that nothing would ever rouse him his eyelids flickered and his lips moved.

'Lucy, Lucy, I want you. Lucy, come here.' The words were a whisper. Then his eyelids flickered again and opened. He looked at Anne, but there was no recognition in them. Again he murmured, 'Lucy.'

Anne sat quite still. Her heart had been touched by icy fingers and the pain was almost beyond bearing but she still held his hand and her voice went on calmly.

'It's all right, Jeff, darling. Don't worry any more. Lucy will be here before long. I promise you.'

Her voice grew even more soft and gentle, like a mother crooning to a sick child, and all the time she told him how Lucy would be with him soon. She had no idea the nurse had gone. Later Sister came back and put an arm round her shoulders.

'Come along, my dear, you've done all you can for now. He's got more than a fighting chance.'

Anne's great eyes turned to hers, and Sister, used to suffering as she was, thought she had never seen more tragedy on a girl's face. So Nurse had been right. He hadn't been asking for this girl at all. Why hadn't they realised her name was not Lucy? He had been muttering it on and off for hours. For one horrible moment she wished that he had died before he put such agony on a girl's face.

Anne made no protest. There was no point. She must go home and put her house in order.

Rosie was waiting for her and for a moment she thought Jeff was dead. She put her arms round Anne, but Anne spoke quietly, as if reading her thoughts.

'It's all right, Rosie, he isn't dead. They say he has much more chance now, but you see he wasn't asking for me. It was his wife he wanted.'

They went home and Rosie took off Anne's coat and sat her in a chair as if she were one of the children. Knowing that Anne never drank tea if she could have coffee she said, 'I'll put the coffee on.'

'No, make tea.' Anne spoke in a whisper. 'Jeff and I always drank coffee and I don't think I ever want any again.'

Rosie knelt by her side. 'Anne, dearest, don't you think you are looking too far ahead? He wasn't really conscious and he may only have used his wife's name because he had used it so often in the past.'

'No, it isn't that. I think he always wanted her even when he didn't know it. I deliberately blinded myself. He was far lonelier than I knew and I love him so much. He loved me all right, but only with a small part of himself. Don't try and soften it, Rosie. I know when I'm beaten. Somehow I must find his wife's address. I'll have the tea and then I'll look.'

But there was no letter from his wife or from his parents anywhere and Anne knew without a doubt that he didn't want them in the house where she was.

'Rosie, I've got to find her, but I don't know how. What shall I do? He needs her so much.'

Dear God, thought Rosie, does this man know what he is losing? She doesn't even care about herself.

'Anne, why don't you wait? Just a few days. Give him time to recover a little more.'

'And have him try all over again to sort himself out? No, he'll fret then and have less chance of getting better. I know what he wants now even if he doesn't realise it. Only a little bit of him has been mine. The rest belongs to his wife. Rosie, have you been reading the papers? I haven't even looked at them. Has there been anything in them about the way Jeff was beaten up?'

'Only just a little paragraph on the first day. Perhaps the police have kept it quiet until he recovers. Hasn't anyone from the paper he sometimes writes for asked about him?'

'I don't know. I haven't seen anyone. Perhaps you are right. Maybe the police are waiting until he can talk to them and don't want too much said about it.'

'What makes you think about that now?'

'Because there is a friend of his, a doctor. I don't know him but if he knew what had happened I am sure he would have been to see him. He is the one I should ask but I only know his name is George. Nothing else about him, not even his surname.'

She began to search through Jeff's little diary. A telephone number, anything. And then she found it. George Masters. There was no address, just the phone number. It was the only George in the book so it must be right.

'I'm going to phone him now.' Rosie knew it was because she was afraid that if she didn't do it at once even her courage would fail.

The quiet voice at the end of the line had only a trace of West Indian accent.

'You're Jeff Anderson's friend, aren't you? I'm a friend of his, Anne Hunter, but I don't suppose you've heard of me.'

'On the contrary. Jeff told me about you. What can I do?'

Briefly she told him of Jeff's condition.

'And you want me to see him?'

'Not only that. I want you to send for his wife. He needs

her. There is enough money in his bank for her passage.'

'And what about you?' It was the quiet voice that made him ask. It was too quiet, unnaturally so.

'I'm all right.'

'Then that's fine. I'll see Jeff.' He did not ask for her address, he didn't want her to know there was something unnerving about her control. Jeff had only told him the road where he lived, not the number, but the hospital would give it to him. Jeff was hovering between spasms of consciousness. George took his hand and said, 'Hullo, Jeff.' The heavy eyelids flickered.

' 'Lo, George, where's Lucy?'

'She'll be here soon, old chap. Just go to sleep.'

Anne was sitting quietly with her hands folded, as if suddenly she had no energy left, no thought, no desire. Rosie looked at the rather small, neatly dressed man with the almost ugly face and was promptly on the defensive for Anne.

'I'm George Masters. May I see Anne Hunter?'

Anne looked at him with big, dry eyes. 'Have you sent for Lucy?'

'Not yet, Anne, but I will.' He looked at Rosie and she stared at him aggressively and it was all he could do not to smile in spite of the tragedy in Anne's eyes. The flaming-haired beauty didn't trust him! Thank goodness Anne had a friend.

'I'm glad Anne has someone with her.' He spoke as if he knew Anne personally and Rosie felt some of the agression lift. In the last hour or so she had wondered what she could do for this quiet, composed Anne, was beyond her. If only she had cried, or been bitterly angry as she had seen her in the old days, but she just sat there, as if waiting for something to happen.

'I've seen Jeff, Anne, and I know why you want to send

for his wife. I think you are right, he needs her but I know what a shock this must be for you.' He had no intention of softening the blow. Better she took it all at once. 'I don't think you know how much he was bewildered by all that has happened. He was blown this way and that, not knowing what to do for the best. He's drifted badly since he came to England and I think you gave him something he needed at the time. I believe he loved you, possibly still does, but not as he loves Lucy. It's going to be damnably hard on you but you must have great courage or you wouldn't have asked me to send for her. Now what are you going to do?'

She looked at him vaguely. 'What do you mean? What can I do?'

'I want things quite clear before I send for Lucy. You have to fade right out of the picture if they are going to make a proper marriage again. It is hardly fair for her to come here and then find another woman. She probably suspects there is anyhow. Women seem to scent these things. I don't want to get her over here and then, as soon as Jeff is better, you come into the picture again and try to break things up between them.'

Rosie was fighting mad. 'How can you be such a brute? Anne has given up everything for him. Hasn't cared about herself at all and you have the nerve to talk to her like that!'

Anne gave a fleeting smile. 'Oh, Rosie, don't be silly. I didn't give up anything. I did what I wanted to, that's all. What he says makes sense.' She turned to George with an amused smile on her lips but her eyes were full of pain. 'Don't worry, I won't break anything up. I just didn't understand until to day, that's all.'

'Then we've got to make plans, haven't we?' He spoke as if it was something they were in together and to Anne it was a lifeline. Until now she had felt helpless, not knowing which way to turn.

'First and foremost she cannot come here, even if you went away. Some kind neighbour would soon tell her. I had better collect all Jeff's things and tell her he moved in the last few weeks or something. Once that is done we can talk about your future.'

It was as if he took over the responsibilities that should be Jeff's and Anne accepted it. She knew that for a time she was incapable of thinking clearly and this was Jeff's friend, who understood him. There was no pity but she could feel his sympathy and Rosie knew he could now do far more than she could. He would give Anne things to do, organise her relentlessly but for her own good.

A couple of days later Rosie went home but said she would be over on her first day off. Anne was going about the business of sorting Jeff's clothes, packing them neatly along with his books and papers. She didn't go to the hospital, knowing she could never see Jeff close again or her will would give way. She left it all to George, not even asking if he had had a reply to the cable he had sent to Lucy.

When George again went in to see Jeff he had regained complete consciousness. He was a ghost of his former self but quite rational and it was obvious that he was on the road to recovery. His great physique would pull him through now.

'It's good of you to come, George. How did you know I was here?'

'Anne told me.'

'Anne! They tell me she spent most of her time here until a couple of days ago but she hasn't been here since. There must be something the matter. Is she ill?'

'No, Jeff, but she won't be coming. I've sent for Lucy.

Anne asked me to. Don't worry about it now. I'll tell you what happened when you are stronger.'

'Don't be a fool! Whatever it is you had better tell me now. It is easier to know than lie and think until your brain swims.'

'Yes, you're right. Anne did spend all her time here but as soon as you began to regain consciousness you asked for Lucy. Anne was here and you didn't even know her. She went home, found my telephone number and asked me to send for her. It is as simple as that.'

'She doesn't want to see me again?' He looked like a scolded child and had it not been that he was a very sick man George knew that he would have struck him. Did he think he could have two women dancing attendance on him?

'If I thought Anne didn't want to see you again I would feel better about it. She has great courage and once she knew it was Lucy you wanted she made up her mind to step out of your life. If you had broken with Lucy and stayed with Anne you would have been haunted by her and the children. In time Anne would have known and do you think she would have been happy? It is better she found out before it was too late. Lucy is coming. Don't be haunted by Anne. It is in the past. You can't have them both even if you want to and I don't think you do. Give Lucy all you have to give and don't let the memory of another woman come between you.'

'Where is Lucy going to stay and what will Anne do?'

'I'm not a fool, leave it to me. I've moved all your clothes to my place and I'll tell Lucy you had to find somewhere else to live but had not yet moved in. I know a tiny flat that will be ready in a few days. In the meantime I am putting Lucy into a hotel.'

'What about money?'

164

'You are determined to cross your bridges, aren't you? I've got your bank statement and your cheque-book. I'll meet current expenses and you can pay me later. You've got enough. Don't worry about Anne. She's a pretty fine girl.' And when you're better, he thought, I shall take the first opportunity to tell you you never deserved her.

He met Lucy at the airport and took her straight to the hotel. He could hardly believe she had altered so little over the years. The same gentle girl he had known, the same sweet smile, the same girl he had loved so much. She hadn't altered at all, but he had. There was anxiety in her eyes, but if she suspected Jeff had not been faithful to her she gave no hint. She'll hold her head high, he thought, pretend she doesn't suspect a thing and get over it that way but I must impress on Jeff there must be no confession to hurt her gentle soul. Her pride would be hurt, too, and he didn't know how she would take that. She loved Jeff but he doubted if she had the great depth of love of which Anne was capable. Anne wouldn't care tuppence about her pride or anything else.

He took Lucy to the hospital and glimpsed the reunion and left, telling Lucy he was sorry he couldn't wait but one of the staff would get her a taxi. He would see her to-morrow. She looked at him gratefully.

'Dear George, you haven't altered a bit.' He grinned. Little did she know how much he had altered, he was only beginning to realise it himself! Then he went to see Anne.

She was struggling desperately with the typewriter which he hadn't yet taken away.

'What on earth are you doing? You don't look very competent.'

'I'm not, unfortunately, but it's Jeff's book. It's almost finished and I know just how he wants it to end and I'm on the last page. I want you to get it properly typed and send it to a publisher. She looked up at him, her eyes dark pools that a man could drown in. 'It's the last thing I shall ever be able to do for him. It's a very good book. When his wife is not there you can tell him. He wouldn't be able to do it himself for some time and if it could be sold he will have the money. I know he will need it.'

'Can you finish it if I sit here quietly?'

She nodded and a half an hour went by while she struggled patiently. Then she pulled the sheet out of the typewriter.

'Now you've done that we had better talk about you.'

'What is there to talk about? Next week I am going back to my job. They haven't given me the sack but they will if I don't go back soon.'

'And what are you going to do later? You're pregnant, aren't you?'

'How did you know? Jeff doesn't, even Rosie doesn't.'

'I don't know. Instinct maybe. Have you people to go to? Can you go back home?'

'I've a cousin in Wales and she would take me in but I can't see her being very pleased. I've never even written to her since I left. I haven't been what you might call the flower of the family. Not that I intend to throw myself on their kindness. Honestly, George,' (she spoke the name easily) 'they were pretty good to me. I realise that now. They all tried to make me see sense but I went my own way, regardless of who was hurt. Now I'll cope by myself. At some time or other I'll write and tell them I'm sorry but not because I want something from them.'

'How long will you be able to stay in your present job?'

'Until it begins to get obvious but they know I'm not married and I don't want to embarrass them.'

'Leave it to me. I'll find you a job and later a home for unmarried mothers. Do you want to keep your baby?'

She stared at him. 'What the hell do you think I am? It's my baby and I'll keep it somehow.'

'O.K., don't snap at me. I'll help as much as possible.'

'Are you doing this for me, or Jeff, or yourself?' Her expression was telling.

'I've no designs on you, if that's what you mean. Because you've lived with one man without being married I don't think you fair game.'

'I'm sorry. I didn't mean it to sound as bad as that. I'll make some tea.'

'Make it coffee.'

He wasn't prepared for the sudden collapse. She wept hysterically with her head on the table and he made no attempt to comfort her, just let her go on crying while he got up and made coffee. He poured it out and put the cup by her shaking body.

'Here you are, Anne, drink it up.'

She lifted her head and looked at it and then swept it off the table with one movement of her thin arm.

'I won't drink coffee, ever again. It was the first thing we ever had together. We always drank coffee.'

It was such a childish reaction that he was staggered. She put her head back on the table and sobbed more convulsively than ever. He cleaned up the mess and looked at her heaving shoulders and suddenly he caught hold of her and shook her.

'That's enough nonsense, Anne. I know you must have been through hell and I know you've covered your pain in a way few women would or could but to behave like this is insane. You've made your point. Part of you is too hurt to be able to make sense but do you think you can go through the rest of your life behaving like a silly child? Are you going to throw coffee at anyone who offers it you?'

He knew it wasn't the coffee but the collapse of a courage

she had driven too hard. The coffee had been the last straw.

'I am going to pour you out another cup and you'll drink it and I'm going to give you a couple of tablets and you are going to bed and there you will stay until I see you in the morning.'

She did as she was told with a quietness that was almost frightening and he waited until she was in bed. When he let himself out of the door she was sleeping. He had the typescript and the typewriter with him. He sat up half the night reading the book. Anne was right, it was good, damn good. Far better than anything he thought Jeff could do. There was strength as well as feeling. Then he knew why. Anne had been the spur, he would never have written such a book without her. He might write other books but this one would probably make his name and later people would wonder why he had never managed to catch such force again. That would be Jeff's loss.

He went to the hospital before surgery. Jeff was propped up against a pile of pillows looking darkly handsome. George knew he would never envy him again. He had talked about doing so much, he might continue to write and make a good living but he would never attain what he wanted, he would always miss out somewhere. The tragedy of a man who lacked something but never knew what. A man who would probably go through the rest of his life wanting what he hadn't got.

'You're looking much better. It won't be long before you are your old self. I came early, Jeff, because there is something I must say. Whatever happens don't start unburdening your soul to Lucy. Confession might ease you but would only hurt her.'

'But I think she already guesses there was someone else.'

'Then let her guess. She will probably only think it was a

light affair, quickly forgotten now she is with you. Never mention Anne. Take Lucy back home as soon as you are fit.'

'What have I got to go back to?'

'That's what I wanted to say. I've read your book.'

'It isn't quite finished.'

'It is now. Anne did it and you can't tell where you ended and she began. It's a good book, Jeff. I may not know much about it but I'm certain I'm right. I'll get it typed for you and give it to an agent I know. If it sells will you promise to go home? There you can forget England.'

'Go home on the money from one book? You don't know how little they make.'

'This one may. I'll do my best to get the *Meteor* interested. They've taken some of your work, haven't they?'

'For a man who knows nothing about writing you seem to be well informed.' Jeff was in a touchy mood.

'For God's sake don't be petty. I didn't come to England yesterday and I can read. I've even written a few bits for medical journals. All right, have it your own way.'

'I'm sorry, George. Seeing Lucy, knowing what I've been doing, makes me realise what a swine I've been to her.'

And what about Anne? George thought, but said nothing. Jeff suddenly spoke of Reggie and his mother, of Lizzie and Alf and the kindness they had shown him, said he would like to see them. This was safe ground, they knew nothing of Anne.

'Then you can jolly well write to them when you feel well enough, or Lucy can. Give her something to do.' George didn't know why he was so angry. Yes, he did, Jeff was already putting Anne outside of his life, not wanting to know how much pain he had caused. For a moment he was tempted to say Anne was pregnant but stopped in time. That was Anne's affair.

When the book had been properly typed he decided to take it personally to the one agent he knew.

First he must see Anne. She was looking more rested but he had forbidden her to go back to work yet. He had rung up the surgery himself and said she was suffering from exhaustion. They needed her but would wait a little longer. Today she had the look of a lost child. Somehow he must jerk her out of the apathy which seemed to have settled on her.

'Go back to work tomorrow instead of waiting until next week. No sense in sitting around and now you're better you want something to do. Get out of this place, too, as soon as possible.'

'And how to find somewhere?'

'You've parted with Jeff and you had better pull yourself together and think of the future, hadn't you? Or did you just make a grand gesture and now regret it?' He walked over to the window and stared out at the grey day. Suddenly he turned and went over to Anne, putting small but strong hands on her thin shoulders. 'All right, Anne, I give in. I realise it is an impossible situation and you do need the father of your child. You can't be expected to cope without him. I was wrong. Go and see Jeff. He'll stand by you.' He knew she would never do it but his words put that bit of fire back.

'Oh, go to the devil and leave me alone. I'll get by without your help. I'll go back to work and start looking for somewhere to live. You needn't bother any more.'

'Don't bite my head off, what a nasty temper!' He smiled. 'I'll tell you now why I've wanted to do so much. It's not only that Jeff and I have been friends most of our lives, it's his father, too. He was the one man who helped and encouraged me. Without him I wouldn't be where I am. He's wonderful man and Jeff is his only son.'

'And the other reason?'

'At one time I was desperately in love with Lucy. She's a kind and gentle creature.'

'And she mustn't be hurt! I don't matter. I'm just a dirty little whore.'

The bitterness and sheer hatred in her voice gripped him.

'Don't be a blasted fool. I'm not blaming you. Jeff behaved like a swine and if he wasn't in the condition he is I might have knocked his teeth in.'

Anne's eyes filled with tears and suddenly she was crying, not the hysterical, overwrought tears he had seen before, but tears of regret.

'It wasn't really his fault at all. I'm the one to be blamed. He was lonely and I fell in love with him. I thought he was in love with me and carried him along with me. I've always known what I wanted and gone my own way. I don't regret for myself so much but I do for him. I'm afraid he'll always hate the memory of me and yet be unhappy for me. He's good and gentle and it will hurt him so much.'

If I wanted to be a brute I'd tell you he is already putting you out of his mind, he thought, but I can't.

'That is something he must face. You can't take all the blame. He's hardly a boy. You have to face the fact that you are going to have a baby without having a husband. Anne, I've read the book and had it typed. You are right. It's good. I'm going to take it to an agent now. Put on your coat and come with me. You can sit in the car. Afterwards we'll have a meal somewhere. I'm not doing any calls today.'

She put on her coat and went with him. Anything to get away from the aching loneliness of knowing that never again would Jeff take her in his arms. George was right. She must leave this place. It was too full of Jeff. His big body seemed everywhere.

171

George didn't bother to talk but his small, neat figure was full of friendliness. She was glad he was pleasantly plain, that he was scarcely any taller than she and his voice was nothing like Jeff's. There was less accent and it had a lighter, almost lilting tone. Nothing like Jeff. She closed her eyes and clenched her hands. Jeff, Jeff, would she ever get him out of her thoughts? Would there come a day in which she didn't think about him? Would this longing ever leave her? It wasn't possible. It was all of her, the best of her. Had she anything left? Could she ever love anyone else? Of course she could, there was Rosie and she would love the baby. It was the only comfort she could find in a world which seemed to have little but pain in it.

11

After that first step forward Jeff's progress was much slower. He would move forward for a day or so and then slip back, lying against his pillows as if even to talk was too much and his great frame seemed to shrink and his dark face faded from the rich, healthy brown to a dirty, greyish shade.

Lucy spent all the time they would allow at his bed, her gentle face calm but her eyes anxious. George's affection for them both never failed but there were occasions when his patience almost did. Jeff was making very little effort to help himself. George thought of Anne in Lucy's place. She would have lost her temper and told him to pull himself together. He found Lucy's sweet patience irritating.

Jeff was able to identify Flashy and the big man from police photographs. They had been in trouble before at Liverpool. When they were picked up they promptly turned Queen's evidence and the smiling white man was caught soon afterwards. The protection racket he had been running was likely to send him down for a nice long stretch apart from the hand he had had in beating up Jeff. The doctors gave permission for Jeff to be taken to court as soon as the trial was arranged but it was clear he was no longer interested in that or his fellow countrymen in England. Any spark of interest he had had been damped right down and George began to wonder if he would ever be quite the same man again.

George talked to the specialist. No, they were sure there was no permanent brain damage, probably just the shock and in time he would make a complete recovery. Time and again George asked himself if he had been wrong in sending for Lucy. Had he been an interfering busybody? Would it have been better had he waited until Jeff was well enough to make up his own mind? If so he had messed up three lives. In those first days he had been convinced Jeff was content to erase Anne from his memory, now he wasn't. Was it the need of Anne that was holding him back?

Lucy was no stimulant to Jeff. Anne would have used her dynamic personality. Lucy waited and hoped, unfailingly gentle.

In the meantime Anne worked with dogged perseverance. She was living with a West Indian couple with two small children and doing her best to be bright and cheerful. At first she spent most of her time in her room, but Laura Grant, with an instinctive knowledge of human nature, sent four-year-old Mary to ask her to come downstairs. She came down with the child's hand in hers. Her own love of children and Mary's friendly disposition began to bring her back to the world of realities. The misery didn't so much recede as her fighting spirit took over.

Jeff was taken to the trial in a wheelchair, but he showed little interest in the proceedings and was taken away before sentences were passed. Anne, with a hat pulled down over her glossy hair, her coat collar turned up, watched from the public gallery and when she left the tears were raining down her cheeks. That pathetic figure in the wheelchair was not Jeff, not the Jeff she knew, or thought she knew. The woman by his side must have been Lucy. Desperately she tried to hate her, but there was little hate left, only a long-drawn-out pain that twisted her stomach and compressed her chest and was so physical that her brain was numb. The hollows in her cheeks grew even deeper and Rosie was frightened. What chance would she have when the baby was born if she went downhill at this rate? She went to see George about it and his manner was so casual she lost her temper.

'She'll be all right.' He was so confoundedly confident and she had no idea how his heart ached. 'Anne has more in her than you think. She's going through a bad patch but she'll pull out of it.'

'And that's all you care!'

'Rosie, stop being idiotic. If we work ourselves into a state it won't help Anne. It's because she has such strength she feels so deeply. Another woman might have gone to pieces, gone to Jeff or Lucy and thrown herself on their mercy but not Anne. She'll pick up the pieces and start again. Sometimes I think I should never have sent for Lucy. I don't know but I doubt if Anne would have been really happy with Jeff once she had heard him asking for Lucy. She would never have been sure of him. It's so hard to answer human problems. I'm worried about Jeff, too, for he isn't doing as well as he should.'

'Jeff, Jeff! It's Anne I'm worried about. As far as I am concerned he can go to the devil where he belongs.' Rosie's eyes glinted with anger.

'If Jeff doesn't pull himself together he is not the only one who will suffer. There are other people involved and it wouldn't help Anne. Rosie, don't you understand I know Anne is worth a dozen Jeffs?' His quiet voice and serious eyes had the desired effect. 'Give her time. Try not to worry. I'll look after her.'

'I'm sorry but she is my friend and I love her. She's so much better than she thinks she is.'

'I know what you mean and, believe me, she'll make something of her life.'

Rosie went away comforted, feeling the strength of this small man, feeling his faith. Dear Anne, such a fool in some ways, in a way she could never be but with such strength that there must be a future for her. Perhaps it would never be an easy one but, with sudden insight, she knew that Anne would not wish it. Anne could hate and love and fight and once she was herself again she would fight for something worth while. I'll live in a contented backwater, she thought, bringing up a family, trying to give them a childhood different from my own, but not Anne. At some time, in some place, Anne will be big, bigger than I know how. Rosie went to meet her Jim with tears and dreams in her eyes and they were not for herself.

Jeff's book was sold and the *Meteor* wanted to serialise it. George gave him the news and his eyes brightened. Lucy was not there and George was glad. He could talk to Jeff frankly for once.

'That means there is enough money to live on while I write another.' He was suddenly self-confident. 'George, have you heard anything of Anne?'

'Yes, she's fine.'

'Do you think she would see me?'

That was too much. 'How bloody selfish can you be? You've got Lucy back, do you want Anne as well?'

'It's not that. I want to see her myself and tell her how sorry I am for all that's happened.'

'Fine! Tell her you never really loved her but she was a passable makeshift while you hadn't got Lucy. While you're about it I should tell Lucy, too. Make sure you hurt everyone to ease your own conscience. Dear God, how stupid can you be! I begin to wonder if you know what loving is. Go back home, Jeff, and work out your own salvation and leave Anne to work out hers. She'll do it because she is worth more than you can ever give her. Go home and write your books and, if you can't find some other job, teach, do anything, learn to live with yourself, which you may find hard, but for God's sake try and be a good husband and father.'

Jeff was silent for a moment. 'I'd like Anne to have some of the money. I've never done a thing for her financially and she helped me quite a lot with the book.'

George looked at him thoughtfully and there was pity in his eyes. He doesn't even know Anne is the book, he thought. He'll never write another like it if he tries till doomsday and he'll never know how much he owes her. Someday, when he finds the words won't come, he'll blame it on the fact that he went back home and the smallness cramps him, or that Lucy can't understand. He'll dream of Anne and eat himself up. No use trying to make him see sense. For one brief spell he will taste a little glory and the glow of success and then slip back into mediocrity.

'She wouldn't want it and you need it for Lucy and the children. No, Jeff, you are not going to see Anne, for her sake and Lucy's but you need not worry. I intend to keep an eye on her.'

Jeff looked at him with sudden understanding and then a smaller side came to the surface, the side that had prevented him from doing so many things he wanted to do and would probably prevent him all his life.

'So Anne has taken the place of Lucy, George? Strange to think you want the women who love me.'

'Goodbye, Jeff, I'll talk to Lucy about your passage home. You will be fit to travel shortly and the sooner you go the better.' George spoke quietly but there was utter contempt in the words.

'George, I'm sorry.' He was, bitterly sorry, knowing himself in that moment more clearly than he had ever done.

George didn't answer but walked out of the room, his small, slim figure stiffly erect, and Jeff, appalled at what he had said, put his head in his hands and wondered if he would ever have peace of mind again. A few minutes later Lucy came in. George is right, he thought, I've got to learn to live with myself and that will be the hardest job of all. He managed a smile.

'Ready to go home, darling, in spite of having seen so little of England? The book is sold and there will be no problem for a time, at least. Perhaps later we may come back for a holiday.'

She put her arms round him. 'I don't think I want to. I don't like what I've seen of England. I'm longing to take you home to the children. That is all I want.'

When I had Anne in my arms I wanted you, he thought, now I have you I want Anne. Will I ever learn?

Jeff and Lucy were going home. Anne knew their flight because she had insisted on George telling her but she didn't tell him she was going to the airport. She knew it was a foolish thing to do but she had to see Jeff go. Until the sea was between them she would always hope that somehow, somewhere, they would be together again. She watched the passengers walk towards the plane, Jeff, his shoulders hunched, walked by Lucy's side. As the aircraft disappeared in the distance Anne turned away, blinded by helpless tears, knowing that part of her had gone with him, wondering how she would cope in the years ahead. A strong arm went round her shoulders.

'Come along, Anne, I'll take you home.'

'How did you know I would be here?'

'Because I am beginning to know you. It's over, Anne, and you've got to live. Jeff would never make an immigrant here. He was a lost soul and you can make something of your life if you've a mind to and I think you have. Until now you haven't thought much about anyone except Jeff and yourself. Now is the time to start.'

'I'm not the sort to make a do-gooder even if I had the opportunity.'

'That's a silly thing to say. You don't even know what you can do yet. First of all I'm taking you to my flat and cooking you a good meal before I run you home. I am also going to give you a lecture for the good of your soul.'

'I don't take kindly to lectures.'

'I know that but I'm not Jeff and I don't need you to boost my ego or give me a spur. I'm more like you. A fighter.'

She gave him a sidelong glance. He laughed.

'Do you still think I have designs on you? Do you think that is why I am taking you to my flat?'

'No, I never did, really. I was just being bloody-minded. But you make me flaming mad at times.'

'Well, heaven be praised for that. It shows you have some feeling for other people even if it isn't the nicest kind.'

He cooked a meal and she ate a reasonable amount because it was easier to do as George said and she was in no mood to fight.

'Anne, what I am going to say is going to hurt, damnably, but it is time someone said it. I know you loved Jeff, probably you always will but there wasn't much reason in it and a good deal of selfishness. I don't think you ever gave a thought to how many people would be hurt. It wasn't just Lucy. There were the children and Jeff's parents. I know this was Jeff's business more than yours but I don't think you gave them a thought. You loved Jeff and nothing else mattered.'

She sat with her elbows on the table, her chin on her hands and she looked down at her empty plate as if she did not hear him.

'Exclusive love to one person never brings complete satisfaction and after a while you would have smothered Jeff with your love. You might have made a man of him but he wouldn't have thanked you and in time you would have wanted more than he had to give. Wanted a man to stand up and fight you occasionally. That book was not Jeff's, although he thinks it was. It was marked right through with your thoughts, your drive, your personality. When he tries to write another he will know and resent it and Lucy will get the backwash.'

'What's this to do with me now?'

'Because it is high time you grew up and stopped thinking of life as a romance between two people with the rest of the world shut out. Look around you. There are a great many of our own people here and they need help. Help to understand a different country and its people. I believe in integration. I believe it is possible although it may take generations. But it won't be done by carrying chips on our shoulders. It can only be done by understanding.'

'And what the hell do you think I can do about it? I've

got enough to cope with. I'm going to have a baby and I'm not even married, remember?' She was angry, furiously angry. 'I'm going to think of me, me and my baby, first, last and always.'

He smiled, remembering Rosie's words. 'She's so much better than she thinks she is.'

'Who are you trying to convince, Anne, me or yourself? What about little Mary Grant? Would you care if she was suddenly alone in the world? Would you pass by on the other side because you could only care for you and your baby?'

There was a startled look in her eyes, as if she suddenly saw another side to herself.

'Don't try to fool yourself, Anne. Give yourself a chance to find out how much you care. You have far more love to give than you know yet.' He paused and let his words sink in.

'Don't waste yourself, Anne, don't waste the strength God gave you. I work among our people, I know their difficulties but I'm no dreamer, hoping for the millennium. It needs to be worked for and I have enough faith to believe that is why we are here.'

'Do you believe in God?' Her big eyes were puzzled. 'Not just because you went to church when you were little but because it is there, deep inside.'

'Yes, don't you?'

'I don't know. When Jeff was so bad I prayed then, desperately. I prayed that if Jeff recovered I wouldn't care what happened to me and I suppose my prayers were answered but I don't know if I really believe. At this moment I'd like to but perhaps what I want is a lifeline. Something to make sense out of a muddle.' Her shoulders drooped and she looked exhausted.

'Don't try and work out the whole of life in too much of

a hurry. Take a day at a time. Anne, this is probably the wrong moment but once in the past I waited for the right one and lost. I know now it was better like that but I was too young at the time to appreciate it. Lucy is the same as she was years ago but I've altered. What I mean is that I'm not carrying a torch for Lucy even if you thought so once. Anne, will you marry me?'

'Do you know what you are saying?'

'Perfectly well and I'm not asking you out of pity but because I've learnt to love you. It won't be easy. We may fight tooth and nail but we could give each other a great deal. Think about it.'

'You've caught me on the wrong foot. I don't know what to say and I won't marry you for the sake of the baby!'

'I'm not asking you to and I don't want an answer now. I want you to meet some of my friends first, to know something of the men and women I love, black and white, I want you to know something of the way I live before you answer. I don't want a woman as an ornament, nor as an adoring handmaiden, but a partner who will stand by my side and share everything.'

'Are you sure you are not trying to save my face and my soul?'

'What sort of a fool do you think I am? I love you and the love is growing. I'd like to be the father of your child and give it a name but unless you can love me I don't want to marry you. But I think you will. We've got a lot in common and I've a feeling that we belong.' He took the handkerchief from his breast pocket, took off his thick glasses and began to clean them, holding them close to his near-sighted eyes. When he put them on again he saw that Anne was smiling.

'What's so funny? The fact that I talk so much?'

'No, seeing you without your glasses I knew you are not

always as cocksure as you sound, that's all.'

'Who is, Anne? It's only fools who are always sure of themselves.' He gave a her a broad, boyish grin. 'I kid myself along a lot of the time. They say most small men do, it's nature's way of compensating. I could never have screwed up my courage to tell you I love you or to ask you to marry me if I didn't pretend to myself that I'm not afraid.'

Through the burning pain of her love and need for Jeff his quiet sincerity was like a cool hand on a feverish forehead. You had no need to wonder or doubt. George knew what he wanted, what he wanted to do. Jeff was her child, the child she carried, George was a man who could hold her hand along a stony road. A candle in the dark! She didn't know yet what she would do. She would have to be sure before she took the outstretched hand but the fact that it was there gave her a spark of hope.

They were still sitting at the table, the crockery pushed to one side. Anne pushed back her chair and stood up, shoulders no longer hunched with weariness but held back with determination. She knew there was a long walk ahead.

'You believe in work, don't you, George? Then let's get on with it. We'll wash up together and then have our coffee.'